# I found a dead body tonight!

"What's wrong?" she asked. "You sound funny."

"I just ran up stairs. I was in the basement. I've been here all evening, doing my homework."

He hoped she bought the lie. She could repeat it to the sheriff if he needed an alibi.

"I just wanted to say hi," she told him. "I miss you."

He sighed deeply. "I miss you, too. It's good to hear your voice."

"Kaz, are you all right?"

*No, I found a dead body tonight!*

Books in the Horror High series
Available from HarperPaperbacks

# HORROR HIGH

## Heartbreaker

### Nicholas Adams

# HarperPaperbacks

*A Division of HarperCollinsPublishers*

## FOR KELLY RUTHERFORD

This is a work of fiction. The characters, incidents, and dialogues are products of the author's imagination and are not to be construed as real. Any resemblance to actual events or persons, living or dead, is entirely coincidental.

HarperPaperbacks *A Division of* HarperCollins*Publishers*
10 East 53rd Street, New York, N.Y. 10022

Produced by Daniel Weiss Associates, Inc.
33 West 17th Street, New York, New York 10011.

First printing: January, 1991

Printed in the United States of America

HarperPaperbacks and colophon are trademarks of HarperCollins*Publishers*

10  9  8  7  6  5  4  3  2  1

# Chapter 1

Wayne Kasden was not worried about entering Cresswell High in the middle of the spring semester. His father had transferred with his job twice before, during his sophomore and junior years. Kaz, as he liked to call himself, was used to being the new kid in school. He always handled the situation with a poise that he had developed over his seventeen years.

Kaz drove through Cresswell in his red Mazda Miata. When he reached the high school, he pulled into the senior parking lot. After he had climbed out of his new car, he stopped to regard himself in the side mirror of the vehicle. He straightened the lapel of his cream-colored linen jacket, pushing up the sleeves on his forearms. Beneath the stylish coat, he wore a bright blue T-shirt. Baggy gray gabardine trousers and tasseled cordovan loafers rounded out his ensemble. He paused to run a comb through his light brown hair.

He was ready for his first day at Cresswell. "Let's see what this burg has to offer," he said to himself, confident that he would find the right kind of companionship and have a good time.

"Hey! You!"

The female voice had come from behind him. Kaz turned to flash his steel-blue eyes at a red-haired girl who was approaching him with an angry look on her face.

"You can't park here," she told him. "It's for—oh!—" She seemed to deflate, losing her anger, forgetting that she had been ready to tell him that the parking lot was for seniors only. Now she was grinning dumbly at the handsome new student who was smiling at her, revealing his perfect teeth.

"Hi, I'm Brandy," she said cautiously.

Kaz squinted at her. "Brandy, huh. What's the problem?"

"Uh, nothing. I've just never seen you before. What's your name?"

"That depends," Kaz replied. "Are you a cheerleader?"

"Yes," she said, pleased.

Kaz flipped on a pair of Ray-Bans. "Too bad."

"Huh?"

"Cheerleaders aren't my type," he replied flippantly. "Too gushy. Take it light, Brandy."

He walked away, strutting toward the front entrance of the school. Kaz didn't go for perky redheads. He preferred girls who were a little more interesting. He left Brandy gaping in disbelief.

As he climbed the steps to the front door of Cresswell High, another group of girls turned to whisper among themselves. Kaz flashed his smile and winked at them.

"Beautiful," Kaz said. "They're all beautiful."

He had wondered about Cresswell. But now he could see that it was going to be a great place to scope the babes. Spring was in the air, and Kaz intended to pluck the April flowers from the green meadow.

He entered the front door. His lean body swaggered down the hall with authority. Kaz kept himself in shape, though he had never been one for sports. He'd never felt compelled to prove himself on the athletic field. Kaz only worried about what it took to prove himself with the ladies.

As he moved toward the school office, he could hear the girls talking behind his back.

"Who's that?"

"Gosh, he's cute."

"A good dresser, too."

"He looks like that guy on television."

"Yeah, the one who plays that cop on *Jump Street.*"

It had been like this at the other high schools he had attended. Why should Cresswell be any different?

Seeing the office ahead of him, he pushed through the doorway and fixed his gaze on yet another pretty girl. He took off his sunglasses to have a better look.

Her long, straight brunette hair was drawn back in a ponytail. She wore a pair of clear-rimmed glasses that gave her a look of intelligence. Something about her was interesting, which immediately made her Kaz's type of girl. If nothing else, she could do his homework for him.

The girl lifted soft brown eyes to look at him. He smiled but she didn't melt. She refused to be stunned by his handsome presence. He liked that.

"Yes?" she asked blankly.

She met his gaze with bold authority. He found himself wanting to stroke her shiny brown hair. He had to find a way to charm her.

"Good morning," he said.

"May I help you?" she asked.

"Yes, I'm Wayne Kasden," he said politely. "I just moved to Cresswell. I'm here to register."

"Oh."

"What's your name?"

She hesitated and then replied, "Marcia."

He tried his killer smile. "I'm lost, Marcia. Out in the ozone. I don't know what to do first. I feel like the kid in *Small Change.*"

Marcia's dour expression gave way to a half smirk. "*Small Change?* You know that film?"

"*L'Argent de Poche,*" Kaz replied in a French accent. "I love Truffaut. Bertrand Blier, too."

Marcia leaned back in her chair. The smirk surrendered to a real smile. "Have you ever seen *Get Out Your Handkerchiefs?*" she asked.

Kaz knew he had her. Bookish girls usually bought the foreign film routine. He'd pegged her accurately. Now he had to close in for the clincher.

He gave her a quizzical look. "*Get Out Your Handkerchiefs?* No, but I've always wanted to see it. Hey, how about *Diva?*"

Marcia nodded enthusiastically. "Sure, I love that one. What did you say your name was?"

"Wayne Kasden," he replied. "But you can call me Kaz."

"Marcia Granholm. You said you need to register?"

4

"That's right," Kaz said softly.

Marcia did all the work for him. In a few minutes the papers had been filled out. When she was finished, Marcia told him where to take the forms and smiled at him from behind the desk.

Kaz breathed a sigh of relief. "You saved my life, Marcia. I wish there was something I could do for you. I'd ask you to the movies, but I wouldn't want your boyfriend to get mad at me."

"Oh, I don't have a boyfriend," Marcia replied. "Not anymore."

"Really? Are you a senior?"

"Yes," she replied.

Kaz thought that she was probably seventeen years old. He liked girls his own age. They were usually more mature.

Kaz smiled warmly. "Say, this really is my lucky day. I don't suppose there's a theater around here that specializes in foreign films."

Marcia shrugged. "Not in Cresswell. But *The Bicycle Thief* is showing at the revival house in Porterville. Three showings on Saturday."

"Why don't you give me your phone number?" Kaz replied.

"Sure, I—"

Marcia frowned suddenly. Kaz felt a hand on his shoulder. He turned to see a hulking boy with a thick neck. The boy's flat face was scowling at him. Kaz tried to smile back at him.

"What're you lookin' at?" the boy said.

Kaz sighed. Sometimes being the new kid had its drawbacks. The inevitable bully confrontation had not taken long to develop.

Marcia stood up behind the desk. "Ricky, leave him alone."

"Is he bothering you, Marcia?"

Kaz brushed the hand from his shoulder. "Friend of yours, Marcia?"

The thick-necked boy snarled. "I'm her boyfriend."

"No, you're not," Marcia replied. "This is Ricky Buller. He *used to be* my boyfriend. The biggest mistake I ever made. Ricky, leave him alone."

Ricky Buller leaned closer to Kaz. "I eat pukes like you for breakfast, pretty boy."

"I'm trembling in my boots," Kaz replied. "Now, what do you say you take it on the arches, apeman?"

"Huh?"

"Oooh," Kaz mocked. "Snappy comeback."

Their eyes were locked. Kaz thought he was going to have to fight him right there in the office. It would not be the first time he had been called out by the school ruffian. But the confrontation didn't escalate into blows.

"Buller!"

Kaz looked over his shoulder to see a hawkish man.

"Uh-oh," Marcia said. "The assistant principal, Mr. Lipton."

"What's the problem here?" asked Henry Lipton.

Kaz shrugged. "No problem, sir. I'm new here. Wayne Kasden is my name. Marcia and Ricky were just helping me register. I still need to get my schedule of classes."

6

The assistant principal was derailed by Kaz's charm. "Oh. Well, wait in the hall until I can set it up. Are you a senior?"

"Yes, sir. My last school was St. John's High School, down in Jacksonville, Florida. My father is an engineer with the electrical plant."

"All right," Lipton said. "Let me take your registration form. I'll get your schedule right away."

"Thank you, sir."

Lipton moved into his private office.

"Thank you, sir," Ricky Buller said mockingly.

"Shut up, Ricky," Marcia said. "Get to homeroom before the bell rings."

"Listen to her," Kaz rejoined. "She's smarter than both of us."

Ricky pointed a finger at him. "Stay away from my girl."

"I'm not your girl!" Marcia insisted.

Kaz grinned at Ricky. "She's not your girl."

The bell rang for the homeroom period. Ricky scowled one last time at Kaz and then stormed out of the office. Kaz turned to look at Marcia. She was embarrassed by the incident.

"I'm sorry," she said, shaking her head.

Kaz waved his hand. "No problem."

Marcia grimaced. "Be careful, Kaz. Ricky can be . . . well, unreasonable. Downright dangerous. I don't know what I ever saw in him. We didn't go out for very long."

"Even feeding time at the zoo can have a certain fascination," Kaz replied. "I'll wait in the hall, like the old Nazi said."

He left the office and leaned against the outer

wall. For a few minutes, Kaz watched the girls as they passed him.

"Kaz?"

Marcia was standing beside him with his schedule.

He took it from her hand. "Thanks. I hope we're still on for Saturday night."

Marcia smiled warmly at the handsome new student. "Sure, Kaz. It's a date."

# Chapter 2

The tardy bell rang as Kaz headed to his first class, senior English. As he neared the classroom, he saw a girl running down the hallway. She was tall, blond, and beautiful. Like Kaz, she was late for first period. Kaz watched as one of her books slipped to the floor. He hurried to help her pick them up.

"Hi," he said in a friendly tone. "I'm Kaz. What's your name?"

Her pretty mouth curled into a sneer of contempt. "What's it to you, pencil neck?"

He felt stung, but he managed to keep his smile. "Hey, I just wanted to help."

She sighed. "My name's Melanie, all right. I'm late."

He watched as she ran off down the hall. Her golden, wavy hair shifted on her back. She was dressed in a smart-looking skirt and a black silk blouse. Kaz felt an immediate attraction to her, especially since she had seemed impervious to his good looks and winning charm. He watched her until she turned the corner.

"What a fox," he whispered to himself.

But he had to get to class. After all, it was his

senior year. He had to graduate if his father was going to send him to college.

When he found the room number for his English class, he opened the door and slipped into the classroom. He had been hoping for a woman instructor, someone he could charm. Instead, a skinny young man with thick glasses turned to glare at him. Kaz could tell by the look on the man's face that he was in trouble.

"May I help you?"

Kaz looked at his schedule. "Are you Mr. Fern?"

"Yes, I am."

"I'm Wayne Kasden. I'm new here. I'm in your class."

Mr. Fern put his hands on his hips. He had a long face, with a crop of unruly black hair atop his head, and narrow shoulders and long, bony hands. He was the kind of teacher who never gave his students a break. Kaz figured he had never been on a date in his life.

"You're late, Mr. Kasden. Very late. And you've already disrupted my class. Not exactly a good first impression."

Kaz grimaced penitently. "Yes, sir. I had to wait for my schedule."

"I don't like excuses," Mr. Fern replied.

"I don't blame you," Kaz said. "But you know how it goes."

"No, I don't know how it goes."

" 'The best-laid plans of mice and men . . . ,' " Kaz offered.

A curious expression came over the teacher's

face. "Oh? Are you familiar with the Cavalier poets?"

Kaz nodded. "Yes, sir. I really like the one about 'stone walls do not a prison make, nor iron bars a cage.' Good stuff."

Mr. Fern seemed to relax. "Well, it appears that we have a scholar in our midst. Find a seat, Wayne. We're studying the romantic poets. Ever hear of Keats or Shelley or Byron?"

Kaz smiled. "Sure." He recited:

*There are seven pillars of Gothic mould
In Chillon's dungeons deep and old.*

"Very good, Mr. Kasden," the now admiring teacher said. "Please take your seat, so we may proceed."

As Kaz turned to face the class, a dark-haired girl caught his attention. She had thick, wanton ringlets spilling onto her shoulders. She was dressed in a black leotard top and a purple skirt. Kaz detected a mysterious glint in her wild green eyes. He decided to sit next to her in the back row.

As he eased into the desk, the girl turned to look at him. When he winked, she smiled back at him. Kaz glanced away, turning to regard the chalkboard. He could feel the exotic girl staring straight through him. But he didn't want to upset Mr. Fern by flirting with her. He knew she could wait until class was over.

"Did anyone ever tell you that you look like Cher?"

Kaz had directed the comment at the dark-haired girl as soon as the bell rang to end first period.

The green eyes turned toward him. "Cher? Really?"

Kaz nodded. "The dark hair especially. Only you look a lot better than Cher. You have a better nose. It's Roman."

"Thank you."

They both rose out of their seats at the same time. He was quick to notice the curves of her full figure. She was striking; not cute, but still gorgeous.

"So your name is Wayne," she said.

He shrugged. "Yeah, but I like to be called Kaz. What do you like to be called?"

"Sally, Sally Thornton."

Kaz looked at his schedule. "Wow, I hope I'm not late again."

"Here," Sally said, bending closer, "let me have a look. Oh yeah, history. Come on, I'll walk you."

Kaz could sense that she was attracted to him. They moved out of the classroom, leaving the watchful gaze of Mr. Fern. He stared at Kaz, perplexed at this strange boy who could recite Byron so glibly.

When they emerged into the hall, Kaz leaned over toward Sally. "What's his problem?"

Sally laughed, shaking her head. "Old Ferny? He's always staring at me."

"Can't blame him there," he replied. "You are great to look at."

She raised a dark eyebrow, looking sideways at him. Kaz immediately picked up on her attitude.

She was strong, not the kind of girl to fall for the helpless routine that Marcia had bought.

"Hey," he said quickly, "you don't have to baby-sit me, Sally. I can find my way to the next class."

Sally frowned at the sudden shift. "No, it's okay."

Kaz smiled. "I don't want you to be late for your class on account of me."

A smile stretched over her coral lips. "Don't worry about *that.*"

They continued down the hall together. Kaz saw Melanie coming toward them. She looked in his direction, but he ignored her. He knew it was great that Melanie saw him with Sally. Girls always became more interested if they saw a guy with someone else.

Kaz turned to Sally. "What is there to do in Cresswell?"

Sally sighed. "Not much, I'm afraid."

"What do you like to do?"

"I'm into music," Sally replied. "I work in a record store on weekends."

"Great," Kaz said. "When I lived in Florida, I saw Bon Jovi and Aerosmith in concert."

"Really?" Sally sighed. "Cresswell's pretty dull."

He smiled. "I bet you aren't dull. I bet we could have some fun if we tried."

She made no reply. "This is your room," she said, motioning to one of many open doors on the corridor.

Kaz stopped, affecting a sincere manner. "When I saw you . . . well, I wanted to ask you out right away. But I guess anyone who looks like you has a couple of boyfriends."

A sly smile spread over her face. "Maybe. But I could make time for a guy like you."

"Are you free Friday night?" he asked boldly.

"Sure. Here, let me give you my phone number."

The bell rang as she handed him a piece of notebook paper. Kaz tucked the paper into his pocket. Sally touched his arm and then moved away, walking down the hall. Kaz thought she moved like a princess.

He went into his next class, introducing himself to the instructor. As he walked back toward his desk, he looked over the girls in the room. He almost stopped in his tracks when he saw the blond girl named Melanie. She glared at him from the other side of the room but looked away when Kaz nodded in her direction.

He thought it was great that they were in the same class. Maybe he would be able to talk to her afterward. But when the bell rang, Melanie hurried out of the room, never stopping to give him a second look.

For the rest of the day, Kaz thought about the slender blond girl. He was looking forward to his dates with Marcia and Sally, but it was Melanie who fascinated him. He knew very little about her, except that she was mysterious and inaccessible. This inspired him even more to pursue the golden-haired fox.

When the final bell rang, Kaz walked toward the

senior parking lot. He figured he had done well to make dates with two girls who were so different. They would not travel in the same circles, would not have the same friends. He could date both of them without either one of them finding out.

His first day at Cresswell had been satisfying, at least in the girl department. As he approached his car, he was not exactly expecting a third conquest of the day. But he quickly rose to the occasion when he saw an attractive, short-haired girl kicking the back tire of a motor scooter.

She had parked the scooter next to his Miata. Kaz stopped for a moment, studying her. She was clad in a leather skirt and a denim jacket with the collar turned up. Henna streaks ran through her short-cropped black hair. Long, red ceramic earrings dangled from her earlobes. Kaz heard her cursing the motor scooter.

"It won't run just because you talk nasty to it," he called to her.

She lifted her flashing, hazel eyes. "Yeah? Says who?"

He tried his best killer smile. "What seems to be the problem?"

"This bike," she replied. "I can't get it to start."

She kicked the back tire again. She wore pink, high-topped sneakers that were tied with sparkling gold laces. Her face was interesting, with well-defined lips and a turned-up nose. A dimple marked the cleft of her prominent chin. Kaz found himself wanting to hold her in his arms. But he had to play it tough if he wanted to come out on top.

"You got a name?" he said brusquely.

"Carol Ledbetter. Okay?"

He stepped forward. "Mind if I have a look?"

Carol shrugged and stepped back. "Go ahead. You couldn't do any worse."

Kaz went over to the bike. He opened a hatch that allowed him to study the engine. He knew a little bit about scooters, but he hadn't really driven one since he was fifteen. He tried to start it by kicking the starter pedal, but the engine sputtered uselessly.

"It could be a fouled plug," Kaz offered.

Carol folded her arms over her chest. "What?" she snapped.

Kaz frowned at her. "I'm trying to help here, Carol. If you don't like it, I could get lost."

Carol's lips formed a sultry pout. "Oh, who cares anyway!"

Kaz decided to turn her around. "Is there a scooter shop in this town?"

She sighed. "There's one off Washington Street."

"Come on," Kaz said. "Let's go buy a new spark plug."

"I don't have any money."

"That's okay, Carol. You can owe me."

He took off his coat, moving around to put down the top on the Miata. When he got in, Carol hesitated. She glared at him with her hazel eyes. She was very appealing in a rough-cut sort of way.

"What's the problem?" Kaz challenged.

"I don't know *your* name," she replied.

"Kaz. Is that okay with you, Miss Attitude?"

She opened the door and climbed in on the other side. "Kaz, huh? What kind of name is that?"

"If you don't like it, tough!"

Before she could respond in kind, Kaz put the Miata into gear and roared out of the parking lot. Carol seemed to ease up a little. She gave him directions to the scooter shop and waited in the car while he bought a spark plug and a cheap socket wrench especially designed for spark plugs.

When he came back to the car, Carol was pleasant to him. "Thanks for helping. A lot of those dweebs at Cresswell don't even talk to me. They think I'm too weird."

Kaz decided to try his best killer smile again. "You kind of remind me of a dark-haired Madonna."

For the first time, her face broke into a pleasant smile. "Yeah?"

"I dig the streaks in your hair," he went on. "You're very attractive."

"Oh. Thanks."

They headed back to the parking lot. Kaz considered Carol another possibility on his hit list. She wasn't the type to be friends with Marcia or Sally. Carol was a loner, the kind of girl who would be easy to date without complications.

As they turned toward the school, Kaz caught a glimpse of the blond-haired girl—Melanie. She was walking into a boutique.

He sighed, wishing he was with the blond goddess.

Kaz guided the Miata into the parking lot, which was empty except for the scooter. He quickly changed the spark plug. The scooter came to life on the first kick.

Carol was surprised. "You really fixed it!"

Kaz wiped his hands on a tissue he had taken from the glove compartment of the Miata. "No sweat."

Carol frowned. "I can't really pay you."

Kaz turned to face her. "Oh, I don't know. I'm new in Cresswell. Maybe you could show me what to—"

"Hey, jerk!"

Kaz and Carol both turned to look at the black pickup truck that had turned the corner. Ricky Buller guided the truck toward them. He had two friends riding in the front seat beside him. Three more goons were sitting in the bed of the pickup. They all got out, forming a circle around Kaz and the girl.

"Be careful," Carol whispered to Kaz.

Kaz kept his eyes on Ricky. "Don't worry, I can handle it."

Ricky scowled at Kaz. "Well, well. Look what we have here. The pretty boy. And no assistant principal to help him."

Kaz's face turned hard-edged in an instant. "Do you want to fight, Buller? Let's do it. You and me, right here."

The scowl vanished from Ricky's face. The hostile retort and Kaz's expression had caught him off guard.

"What's the matter?" Kaz asked bravely. "You

*18*

afraid to face me without some help from your buddies?"

Carol moved closer to Kaz, putting her hand on his chest. "Leave him alone, Kaz. You don't know what you're getting into."

Kaz gestured toward the circle of boys around him. "If he's so tough, why does he need these guys to back him up?"

"I don't need any help to take you, pretty boy!"

Kaz squared his shoulders. Ricky rushed at him, swinging a forceful right hand. The blow grazed Kaz's chin. Kaz fell backward against the car. Ricky lunged again, but Kaz managed to step out of his way. Ricky's momentum carried him against the hood of the Miata.

Ricky's back was turned to Kaz. Kaz grabbed Ricky's left wrist. He shifted his own weight, pulling Ricky's arm backward. They all heard a snap as Ricky's arm bone popped out of the shoulder socket. Ricky cried out in pain, his arm dangling helplessly by his side.

One of the other boys moved in to defend Ricky. He swung a wild haymaker at Kaz. Kaz ducked the blow and threw a side kick into the boy's groin. The boy went down on one knee, screeching with pain.

Kaz stepped backward, shielding Carol. A maniacal glint flashed in his steely blue eyes. Sweat had soaked through his blue T-shirt.

"One at a time or all together," Kaz said. "It doesn't matter. Anybody else want a piece of me?"

Nobody did.

Ricky Buller staggered toward the truck. "Get me to the hospital!" he pleaded.

Carol looked at the other boys. "Hey, you guys were the ones who asked for it! Help him!"

They dragged their wounded friend toward the pickup. The boys shot hostile looks at Kaz as they drove away, but none of them said a word. Kaz turned to see Carol staring at him. He was glad that it was over and that he didn't have to fight any of the others. Altercations are always misrepresented afterward, and he wanted to avoid getting a bad reputation.

"Are you okay?" Carol asked.

Kaz nodded.

"I thought they were going to demolish you, but you showed them," said Carol.

Kaz sighed, trying to breathe deeply and calm himself down. "I—I can't stand guys like that. They always think they're so tough."

"They're idiots." Carol moved closer, facing him. "Hey," she said suddenly.

"What?" Kaz looked into her sparkling eyes.

Suddenly she threw her arms around his neck. Her lips pressed against his mouth. Kaz felt her warmth. He kissed her back for a long time.

Carol finally broke away.

He grabbed her and kissed her again.

When they finally broke off the second time, Carol looked at him with her hazel eyes. "Kaz, you're something."

"Hey," he replied. "What are you doing tonight?"

# *Chapter 3*

As Kaz drove home toward Rocky Bank Estates, he considered his first day at Cresswell High. Despite his successes with the ladies, Kaz was still a little shaken by the fight with Ricky Buller. Kaz had studied martial arts for two years in Florida before his family moved to Cresswell. And even though Ricky had deserved the beating, Kaz didn't feel right about hurting him. Win or lose, Kaz never felt good after a fight. He didn't want to have a bad reputation.

He shuddered, shaking off the coldness in his shoulders. Kaz had reasons to be elated about his new school, namely Marcia, Sally, and Carol. Carol's hot kisses had left him wanting more. She had been the biggest surprise of the day when she jumped on him in the parking lot. He hadn't expected things to heat up so quickly.

"Carol," he said with a smile. "Punky little Carol."

He had come to her rescue with the scooter, and he had demonstrated that he could defend himself. How could she have resisted him after that? He hadn't really pressed her for a date. It had simply happened, the force of Cupid's hand.

"Carol, Marcia, and Sally. Good things happen in threes—or is it bad things?"

The wind whipped through his sandy hair as he guided the Miata past Pelham Four Corners, toward the entrance of Rocky Bank Estates. Kaz liked the new neighborhood. Willows and maples lined the streets in front of well-tended lawns and flower gardens. His own house, which he and his parents had just moved into, was a light yellow, three-story clapboard structure with bay windows and overhanging eaves, set on three-quarters of an acre. It was a welcome relief from the boring condo in Florida.

He pulled into the driveway and got out of the car. His mother was home. She greeted him as he walked through her door. He kissed her lightly on the cheek and gave her a big smile.

"You're a little late, Wayne."

"Hi, Mom. I was helping a friend with a motor scooter."

She smiled warmly. "You've made a friend already. That's nice. You know how much I worry about you. We've moved so much."

"Sure, Mom."

Her smile eased a bit. "You've got blood on your chin. What happened?"

Kaz touched the slight abrasion where Ricky's fist had grazed him. "Oh, I must have bumped it when I was fixing the scooter."

"What's your friend's name?"

He hesitated. "Uh, Carol."

"A girl. That's nice. You always seem to have

girlfriends. Dinner's in an hour, honey. Your dad is working late so it will just be you and me."

"That's great, Mom. I'm going upstairs to wash up."

Kaz climbed the steps to the second floor. He threw his books on his desk and then hung up his linen coat. He always took care of his clothes. He liked to look good. The girls appreciated it, and his parents could afford it.

When he had washed his hands, he studied his face in the mirror. The cut on his chin was barely a nick. He treated the cut with an antiseptic cream. The abrasion wouldn't mar his handsome face.

He went back to his room, falling on the bed. He took out several pieces of paper, the phone numbers from the girls. He picked up the phone. Kaz's parents always let him have a private line. They trusted him to be responsible.

"Who's the first lucky contestant on *Wheel of Kaz?*"

He punched the numbers on the touch-tone.

"Marcia Granholm, please. Marcia? Hi, it's me, Kaz. . . . Yeah, I'm fine. . . . I wanted to thank you for helping me this morning. . . . Sure, I found all my classes. . . . All right, I guess. . . . Mr. Fern? No, he wasn't any trouble. I handled him. . . . Sure, I'll hang on."

He waited while Marcia looked for a newspaper. He thought about her long, shiny brown hair. He liked her quiet, thoughtful demeanor. Marcia finally came back on the line.

"Saturday night, *The Bicycle Thief.* Great! . . . Sure, I'll pick you up at seven. . . . An hour to

Porterville? How about six? . . . Great. Listen, I'll drop by the office in the morning and you can give me directions to your house. . . . Gaspee Farms? No, I've never heard of it, but I'm sure I can find it. . . . Okay. I can't wait to see you again, Marcia. Bye."

He hung up, sighing contentedly. Marcia was a brain. She would give him intellectual stimulation, among other things.

"Our next contestant is Miss Sally Thornton." He dialed her number. Her mother answered and explained that Sally was working this evening, filling in for someone who was sick. Kaz was disappointed. He didn't like anything interfering with his plans. Maybe he would go by the mall to see her where she worked. Wasn't it a record store? A visit would really surprise her.

He saw her green eyes flashing at him. Sally's dark curls were a real turn-on. There was poetry in the way she wore the tight-fitting leotard.

But there was one more call to make. "Carol Ledbetter please. Carol? Hi, it's Kaz. . . . Yeah, I just wanted to call to make sure we're on for tonight. . . . What are you in the mood for? . . . Your house? . . . What about your parents? . . . Oh, just your mom. . . . She works nights?"

Carol gave him her address, and he agreed to be at her house at eight that evening.

Kaz hung up, exhaling as he leaned back on his bed. Carol was turning out to be the real catch. Her mother worked nights so she would be available on weeknights. He could put her off on the weekends, freeing him to spend time with the others. She came from a single-parent home, so there wouldn't be any father around to give him grief. Carol was a great kisser, too.

He could still taste her lips. Feel her body pressed against him. Her arms had felt good around his neck.

"Oh, my baby, Carol."

She looked so wild in her denim jacket. The henna streaks in her hair really gave her an exotic image. Kaz figured the other boys at Cresswell must have been pretty lame not to pick up on a babe like Carol.

He jumped off the bed. He had to get ready for their date. Looking good required a lot of time and effort. Kaz wanted Carol to be impressed. He had to turn her on if she was going to stay hot for him.

"Not a bad day at all. Who needs creeps like Ricky Buller when I have my sweet honey Carol?"

In the confusion, Kaz had forgotten all about Melanie, the blond goddess who had dropped her books. He was thinking about the girls who really liked him. He wouldn't think of Melanie again until he saw her in the mall, when he stopped by the record store to see Sally, on the way to Carol's house.

"Hi, Sally. Remember me?"

Sally stood behind the cash register in the record store. She lifted her devastating green eyes and smiled.

"Hi!" she said sweetly. "Where did you come from?"

Kaz shrugged. "I called your house. Your mom

told me you had been called into work. I thought I'd drop by and say hello."

"That's my aunt," Sally replied. "My father is dead. My mom lives out in Seattle."

"She sounded nice," Kaz replied.

Sally nodded. "Yeah, she's cool. She lets me do whatever I want as long as I keep my grades up."

Kaz gave a triumphant yell inside. Sally was perfect. No adult supervision. She would be free to spend time with him.

"Well," Kaz said, "I guess I better go. I wouldn't want you to get in trouble with your boss. I just wanted to say hi."

"Stick around," Sally replied. "I got called into work because one of the girls was sick. I've got a break coming up. Wait a minute and we can go have a slice of pizza."

"Sure," Kaz replied. "I'm ready."

She moved away to help a customer. She was now wearing a burgundy leotard and a black-and-green paisley skirt. Her curves shifted beneath the tight fabric of the leotard. With the dark curls spilling down her back, she couldn't have been more beautiful.

*Kaz, you're the luckiest guy who ever lived*, he thought.

There were eight or nine customers in the store, so Sally would be busy for a while. She was on duty with one other clerk. Kaz decided to study the records, tapes, and CDs.

He glanced at his watch. It was almost seven. He would be cutting it close if he wanted to spend time with Sally and then make it to Carol's by eight. That was part of the thrill. He loved to see what he could get away with.

When Kaz looked up again, he caught a glimpse of shimmering golden hair on the other side of the store. His heart jumped and a tingle ran through his lean body. He was sure the golden waves of hair belonged to the girl who had dropped her books in the hall.

*Melanie!*

He maneuvered around the aisles until he could see her without her seeing him. She was as beautiful as Venus in the Botticelli painting he had studied last year. Kaz moved around a record bin in order to keep her in view.

Melanie was slipping a compact disc into her purse. Kaz couldn't believe it. She was shoplifting. She wheeled around suddenly to look at him.

Kaz nodded, trying to smile. But Melanie's lovely face looked hard and stern. She didn't seem to notice him. She turned away and walked briskly toward the entrance of the store.

"Wait!" Kaz hissed softly so Sally wouldn't notice.

He hurried toward Melanie. He knew the records, tapes, and CDs were equipped with a security device that would set off the alarm if someone tried to steal them. Melanie ignored him. She bolted through the entrance of the store, setting off the alarm. Kaz watched as she quickly disappeared into the crowded mall. He found himself relieved that she had escaped so easily.

Sally, who had been in the back of the store,

came running toward the front. She peered into the throng. But Melanie was nowhere to be seen.

Kaz stepped up next to Sally. "What happened?" he asked innocently.

"Oh, some shoplifter. They always wait until we're in the back. Then they get away even with the alarm. They know they can do it when we're busy. Did you see who it was?"

Kaz shook his head. "No, I didn't see him."

A sigh escaped from Sally's chest.

"Are you going to call security?" Kaz asked.

He held his breath waiting for the reply. He didn't want Melanie to get into trouble. Somehow it didn't matter that she was a thief. He just wanted to get close to her.

"No," Sally replied. "It won't do any good. But maybe we shouldn't go out for pizza. We're busy now, and I should stay in the store."

He turned on his best smile, taking her hand in a gentlemanly fashion. "Sure, I understand."

She smiled back. "You're the best. Cresswell could use more guys like you. Are we still on for Friday?"

"Wouldn't miss it for anything."

Sally looked cautiously over her shoulder before she gave him a peck on the cheek. "See you then, Kaz."

"I can't wait," he replied sweetly. "I just can't wait."

All the way to Carol's house, Kaz was thinking about Melanie's shoplifting escapade. Why was such a beautiful girl stealing from a record store?

The incident should have made him wary of Melanie, but instead he found himself drawn to her even more. He wanted to know everything about her, to find out what was going on inside her head. He saw himself pulling her slender body close to him, pressing his lips to her firm mouth.

Kaz sighed and stared through the windshield of the Miata. The streets were dark in the Upper Basin. He had to squint to see the house numbers. The Upper Basin was rough, dumpy, and cramped compared to Rocky Bank Estates.

He finally found Carol's address. His mood was somber as he strode up the front steps. The blond girl was on his mind. But then Carol opened the door, and Kaz forgot all about Melanie.

Carol stood on the threshold, smiling at him. She was dressed in a long, pink T-shirt dress that clung to her body. The sweet scent of her perfume wafted on the cool night breeze.

Kaz was stunned. "You look great," he said.

She stared at him meaningfully. "Come on in," she replied.

He entered the dark hallway. Carol closed the front door and then leaned back against it, as if to prevent anyone from intruding upon them. Her hand brushed the black, henna-streaked bangs from her forehead.

"I'm glad you came, Kaz," she said.

"So am I."

Kaz felt a tightness in his chest. His whole body was tingling. He wanted to wrap his arms around her. But he had to play it cool, to make sure the feelings from the afternoon were still alive.

He held out his arms. She moved toward him, putting her hands on his shoulders. Kaz lowered his face, touching his lips to the soft nape of her neck. Her clean, sweet fragrance intoxicated him. The fire welled inside him. He could barely catch his breath.

Carol pressed against him, burying her face in his chest. Her arms wrapped around his slender waist, and he could feel her heartbeat.

"You helped me today," she said softly. "Nobody ever helps me."

"It was nothing," he replied. "You needed me."

"I still need you, Kaz. More than you know."

He stroked her hair. Finally Carol took his hand and led him into the living room. The furniture was old and worn, but the room was neat. They sat on a sofa. Carol switched on the remote, and the television sprang to life, but they didn't look at the bright screen.

Carol's gaze was expectant as she looked into Kaz's blue eyes. He held her hand, kissing the tips of her fingers.

"I like you, Kaz."

He felt a little guilty. "Carol, are you sure this is okay with your mom? I mean—"

"She doesn't care," Carol replied. "Not at all. She lets me do whatever I want."

"I don't want to get you into any trouble."

"You won't, Kaz. You won't."

"You're so beautiful, Carol. I—"

She grabbed him, the same way she had grabbed him in the parking lot. She pressed her lips to his mouth, kissing him hard. He could hear a soft, urgent moan deep in her throat when he kissed her neck.

"Oh, Kaz, no one has ever made me feel the way you do."

Kaz wrapped his arms around her and held her close.

The next day at school, Kaz was surprised to find that Melanie was in his homeroom. He tried to smile at the slender, blond girl, but she only smirked and turned away. She probably thought he wanted to give her a hard time. But Kaz just wanted to talk to her, to get to know her better. Even after the hot time with Carol, he still found himself drawn to Melanie.

He was trying to get her attention when the announcement came over the loudspeaker. "Wayne Kasden, please report to the assistant principal's office."

Kaz frowned, feeling the bottom drop out of his stomach. He saw Melanie turn to look at him. But it was too late to flirt. He had to get up and leave the room with everyone watching him.

When he had reached the office, he saw Marcia behind the desk. "What's up?"

Marcia had a concerned look on her face. "Did you fight with Ricky Buller?"

Kaz grimaced. "Oh, no."

Marcia put her hand on his forearm. "What happened?"

"I kicked his butt," Kaz replied.

Her eyes grew wide. "Really?"

Before he could reply, Mr. Lipton burst out of his office. "In here, Kasden."

Kaz went into the office, taking the seat on the other side of the assistant principal's desk. "Good morning, sir."

Mr. Lipton focused his hawk eyes on him. "What's this about your dislocating Ricky Buller's shoulder?"

Kaz was trembling, but he tried to stay cool. "He came after me in the parking lot. I defended myself. Ask Carol Ledbetter. She was there. She saw it all."

"I figured as much." He sighed. "I don't blame you, Kasden. I figured Buller had it coming. The baseball coach is complaining. Buller was his star left-handed pitcher until you took care of that."

"Sorry."

The bell rang for first period.

"Okay, Kasden, you're free to go. I can handle the baseball coach. But try to stay away from Buller. You're new here. It's best not to get a reputation too soon. There will always be someone gunning for you."

"Yes, sir. Thank you, sir."

When Kaz came out of the office, Ricky Buller was standing in front of Marcia's desk with his arm in a sling. Kaz ignored his scowl. He winked at Marcia and told her that they were still on for Saturday night.

"I'm not finished with you, pretty boy," Ricky Buller said.

Kaz walked away from him, heading for English

32

class. Sally was there. She seemed impressed. The whole school knew that he had punched out Ricky.

Later, Kaz saw Carol in the hall on the way to second period. Kaz told her that he had a great time with her and he wanted to see her again soon. Then he saw Melanie in history class.

Melanie kept looking at him, but she ignored his efforts to talk to her after class. Kaz knew he would wear her down sooner or later.

# Chapter 4

By Friday night, Kaz was ready to go out with Sally. He had spent the whole week juggling the three girls, as well as trying to get Melanie to talk to him. But the slender, blond-haired girl wouldn't give him the time of day, so he turned to his green-eyed girlfriend for a diversion.

He picked up Sally in his Miata. Sally wore a burgundy silk blouse, a plain, cream-colored cotton skirt, and a lace shawl around her shoulders. Multicolored feather earrings dangled from her earlobes.

"You look wonderful," Kaz said with a smile.

She smiled back at him. "So do you."

Kaz wore a leather bomber jacket over his sports shirt. He also wore an expensive pair of cowboy boots that he had specially ordered from a place in Oklahoma.

"Where are we going?" he asked her.

Sally grinned mysteriously. "It's a surprise."

She directed him through the streets of Cresswell. They ended up in an old section of town. The neighborhood was dark and full of red brick warehouses. The place made Kaz a little wary.

"Come here often?" he said, trying to hide his nervousness.

She looked sideways at him. "I thought you liked adventure."

"I like anything as long as I'm with you."

She touched his shoulder. "We're almost there. Just a few more blocks."

Kaz saw the other cars ahead. They parked on the street. He locked up the Miata, wondering if it would be there when they got back.

As they approached the blue door, Kaz could hear the thumping of a bass guitar. Sally knocked on the door. They waited for a moment.

"What is this place?" Kaz asked.

"A private club," Sally replied. "I know the band."

Kaz frowned. "Do I need ID?"

"Don't worry," Sally replied. "It's an alcohol-free club. And I'll pay my share of the cover charge."

"No, I'll get it."

The door opened. Kaz paid the doorman twenty dollars. They walked into a smoky club that was full of tables. The music was blasting loudly. Kaz saw the name of the group on the bass drum: The Charm Mutants.

"You like it?" Sally asked.

Kaz nodded, even though he really hated the place. But he knew he had to pretend to have a good time. He wanted to get closer to Sally. And that meant pulling off the act. They sat down at a table and ordered sodas.

The music was deafening. Kaz liked rock, but

this sounded more like building demolition. But he sat there with a dumb smile on his face, watching the way Sally shifted in her chair. She was worth the wait, he decided. The band finally took a break.

"I'm going to talk to my friends," Sally said. "Do you mind?"

Kaz shook his head. "Anything you want."

He was unhappy to be left alone. Kaz liked to be in control at all times. But soon enough he realized why she had left him. When the band got up to play again, Sally took her place at the front microphone. She winked at him from the stage and then started to sing a lovely, soft ballad. Unfortunately the back-up music sounded more like an eighteen-wheeler downshifting.

Sally was certainly better than the rest of the band. She came off the stage, glowing after her number. They finished listening to the set. Kaz was relieved when Sally said she was ready to go. He tried not to show his pleasure at leaving the club, since he wanted her to think he had enjoyed the loud music.

"Let's go to my place," Sally said.

Kaz wondered if he had blown it with her. Had she seen through his act? She knew he had hated the club. Was she trying to put an end to the evening?

"You were really good," he told her.

"Yeah? The band wants me to go with them full-time, but I don't think they're that good. What do you think?"

Kaz shrugged. "Well, you would make them better."

"You're full of it, Kaz."

He pulled up in front of her house. "Home
sweet home."

Sally turned toward him. "Come on, I want to
show you something."

"I thought I was full of it."

"Yeah, but I like that in a guy."

They got out and went into the house. They
tiptoed up the stairs to Sally's room. It smelled of
incense and potpourri. When they were inside,
Sally closed the door and turned to Kaz.

He saw a strange look on her face. "What?"

She moved toward him, running her hand over
his forearm. "I've been wanting to touch you all
night. Kiss me."

Kaz was pleasantly surprised. He took her into
his arms, touching his lips to hers. Sally seemed to
come alive. She pressed her body against him. She
was hot now.

Kaz forgot all about the rock club. The evening
had finally taken a turn in his direction. Kaz was
starting to have a good time.


Marcia Granholm was nervous about her date
with Wayne Kasden. He was the best-looking boy
she had ever been out with. Much better looking
than Ricky Buller. Kaz was a gentleman, not a
thick-necked goof.

She studied herself in the mirror. She had chosen a gray-and-blue cotton dress. Sitting again at
her vanity table, she began to run a brush through

her long, brown hair. Marcia applied very little makeup. She wanted to appear natural. She had never been comfortable around girls who used too much hairspray and makeup.

Her soft face stared back at her from the mirror. "Oh, Marcia, I hope he likes you."

She knew she liked him. She had been waiting a long time for someone like Kaz. And of all the girls at Cresswell, he had chosen her!

She studied herself more closely, wondering if she should put on a little more lipstick. Would he try to kiss her? Well, if he *really* liked her, he would wait.

What would they talk about? She shouldn't worry about that. Kaz seemed to be comfortable talking about the things she liked. What a coincidence that they both liked foreign films. It was going to be wonderful.

She *did* want him to try to kiss her. But then she wanted him to understand when she didn't kiss him. It was not a game; it was just the way she felt.

"You look fine," she told herself.

Then the doorbell rang and she felt nervous again.

"I really like your car," Marcia said. "It's so cute."

Kaz smiled at her. "I hoped you'd like it."

They headed north on the interstate highway, making for Porterville. Kaz had rested all day Saturday so he would be fresh for their date. Sally had kept him up late the night before. He had gotten home well after midnight, though his parents hadn't found out.

Marcia adjusted her clear-framed glasses. He liked her conservative dress, which was buttoned all the way to the neck. She was not as funky as Sally or Carol, but her shimmering brown hair and smooth face made her just as appealing. She had a lot of class.

Kaz had dressed accordingly. He wore a dark blue blazer, tan slacks, a white shirt, and a blue, red, and green repp tie. He wanted to look like an honor student for his intellectual date.

"You look great tonight, Marcia."

"Thanks. So do you."

She leaned back a little. "How are your classes going?"

Kaz shrugged. "Fine. Mr. Fern just assigned our term paper. We have to choose one of the five topics he gave us."

"I'd love to help," Marcia replied. "Why don't you come over next week and we can get started."

"What about your parents?" Kaz asked. "I mean, I wouldn't want to get in the way."

"It's just my father and me," Marcia replied. "Besides, I have a study over the garage. You wouldn't be in the way."

Kaz felt the old familiar tingle. He couldn't believe his luck. Her own study! They could really have some fun.

"Here's the exit," Marcia said.

Kaz pulled off the main highway, heading into Porterville. He parked on the street near the old theater, which was called the Rialto. He frowned when he saw a line of people at the box office.

"I hope we can get in," Kaz said. "I've always wanted to see *The Bicycle Thief.*"

"I don't think there'll be a problem."

They hurried to the back of the line. A short time later they got their tickets and then found seats in the middle of the theater. When they were settled, Marcia offered to get popcorn and soda. Kaz stayed behind to hold their seats. He sat there, looking toward the front of the theater. It was then that he saw Melanie sneaking in under the EXIT sign.

The door opened slowly. Melanie slipped through, entering without paying for a ticket. She had jimmied the door with some sort of tool that she put into her large purse. She looked gorgeous in her jeans and a beige coat, with the collar turned up.

Kaz found it hard to catch his breath. He always felt anxious when he saw the slender beauty. She sat down in a seat near the front, staring straight ahead. She hadn't seen Kaz. He wondered why he never saw her with a boy. Surely anyone who looked like Melanie could have her pick of the guys at Cresswell.

Suddenly the usher started moving quickly down the aisle toward Melanie. Now he was pointing the flashlight in her face and appeared to be giving her a hard time. Kaz saw his chance to help her. But he had to be fast.

Rising, he took off his blazer and draped it across the seats that he and Marcia had claimed. Marcia wouldn't be back for a few minutes. It was time to come to Melanie's rescue.

He approached the irate usher. "What seems to be the problem?"

The usher gave him a hostile look. "Stay out of this, chief."

Melanie was gazing up at him with her devastating eyes. She was the most beautiful girl in Cresswell. He couldn't resist her.

Kaz had to take control. "First of all, my name isn't 'chief.' Secondly, I don't appreciate your hassling my date."

The usher sneered. "If she's your date, why doesn't she have a ticket stub?"

"Maybe she lost it."

"Then she has to pay again," the usher replied.

Kaz reached into his pocket, taking out a ten-dollar bill. "No problem. Here, take this, in case there's any more confusion. Keep the change."

The usher was instantly apologetic. "Hey, I'm sorry. I—"

Kaz waved him off. "Just go. I wouldn't want to have to tell your boss that you were rude to my girl."

The usher moved away, pocketing the ten dollars.

Melanie was still looking up at Kaz. Her expression had softened. He smiled at her.

"Thanks," she said blankly.

Kaz shrugged. "It's okay." He turned to look for Marcia, but she had not yet returned.

Their eyes met. Kaz felt the tightness in his

chest. She was almost too beautiful. And exciting. He had to get close to her.

"I'm with someone tonight," Kaz said. "What are you doing tomorrow?"

Melanie shrugged. "Nothing really."

"Let's get together," he offered.

He held his breath, waiting for her reply.

Melanie exhaled and folded her arms. "I guess I owe you."

An angry expression spread over Kaz's face. "Hey, don't do me any favors." He started to move away.

"Wait," Melanie said. "Call me tomorrow. I'm in the book. Kaylor on Tidewater Road."

He went back to his seat, putting on his blazer. Marcia arrived with the popcorn just as he was easing into the chair. He was excited, but he had to be cool so Marcia wouldn't notice that he had just met someone else.

"I hope you like butter," Marcia said.

Kaz smiled. "Sure."

"The line was horrible. I never thought there would be this big a crowd, even on a Saturday. . . . Kaz?"

"Huh? Oh, sure, I didn't think there'd be so many people either."

He couldn't stop himself from glancing in Melanie's direction. She even looked back at him once.

"Oh, no," Marcia said. "There's that trashy Melanie Kaylor. Do you know her?"

Kaz shook his head. "No."

"Count yourself lucky. She's bad news."

When the film began, Marcia leaned closer to him.

On the way back to Cresswell later that night, Kaz tried to put Melanie out of his mind. He took Marcia home. They stopped in front of her house. Kaz bent over and kissed her lightly on the cheek.

Marcia smiled and stepped back, making it clear that any further advances were unwelcome.

"What's the matter?"

"I have to get to know a boy before I can feel affectionate," Marcia replied.

Kaz sighed and looked upset.

"Well, if that's the only thing you want from a girl, you should go out with someone like Melanie."

*Not a bad idea,* Kaz thought.

He had been hoping for an invitation up to Marcia's room. Instead, she had presented him with boundaries. Kaz got out of the car, opened her door, and ushered her to her front door.

"I had a lovely time," Marcia said. "I hope we can do it again real soon."

"Sure," Kaz replied. He was ready for a challenge any time.

From the living-room window, Marcia watched him drive away. She thought he was handsome and sort of sweet. But there was something distant about him. He was too stuck on himself. Maybe she could find the depth there. Maybe she could reform a guy like Kaz.

After he drove off, Marcia went upstairs to the den where her father was watching a sports program on television.

"Hi, honey. Did you have a good time?"

"Yes," she said with a sigh. "It was nice."

She went to her room and switched on the light. Marcia felt a bit sad and lonely. Maybe she should have kissed him good night. That was what he wanted. That was what all boys wanted. At least he hadn't pawed her like Ricky Buller. She'd had to fight off Ricky on their few dates together. She kept hoping he would change, but he never did.

Marcia lay on her bed, looking at ceiling. She wondered if she would ever meet a nice boy. Maybe there was still a chance with Kaz. She began to cry, sobbing softly in the silent loneliness of her bedroom.

"I'm really surprised you called me, Kaz."

Melanie sat next to him in the Miata.

"Why's that?" he asked.

"I saw you with Marcia last night," Melanie said. "Miss Perfect. I hate her."

Kaz shrugged. "She's just a friend."

It was a warm, bright Sunday afternoon. Kaz had called Melanie that morning. He just couldn't stay away, especially after the dud date with Marcia.

Melanie wore crisp white slacks and a lightweight blue sweater. A yellow headband kept her hair from being totally unkempt in the wind. Kaz couldn't keep his eyes off her.

Even though Melanie had accepted his offer of a picnic, Kaz still didn't want to seem too eager. Yet Melanie made him feel oddly out of control. On his suggestion, they were heading for a place called Fancy Creek, near Storm Lake.

"What kinds of sandwiches did you bring?" Kaz asked.

Melanie shrugged. "None yet. Pull into the Midway. They've got a good deli. It's just up the road."

Kaz guided the Miata into the parking lot. They got out and went into the supermarket. Kaz followed Melanie to the cooler where the ready-made sandwiches were stored.

"What do you like?" she asked Kaz.

"Anything but olive loaf."

She laughed. "You're funny. Okay, stand behind me. There."

Melanie looked in both directions. Since it was Sunday, the store was understaffed. She began to stuff sandwiches into her large purse. Her hands were quick and practiced.

Kaz's eyes grew wide. "What are you doing?"

"Be quiet. We don't want to get caught."

A nervous laugh escaped from his lips. He should have been angry, but instead he felt a sense of exhilaration. Melanie was irresistible. When her purse was full, they moved toward another aisle.

"What now?" he asked.

Melanie winked at him. "We need potato chips and soda."

"Are you going to swipe those, too?"

"No. You always buy *something*. At least in a grocery store."

She picked up a bottle of generic cola and a big bag of potato chips. Kaz fought back his guilty grin as they went through the checkout line. He paid for the soda and the chips—grand total, two twenty-five.

"Not bad," Melanie said when they were back in the car. "A picnic for under three dollars."

When they were back on the road, Kaz looked sideways at her. "Melanie, why are you always—I mean, do you have to steal those things?"

"No," she replied nonchalantly. "I just do it. I can't seem to help myself. Sometimes I hear a little voice inside telling me to get more and more."

"I guess it's never boring with you around," Kaz offered.

She glared at him. "Why did you go out with Miss Perfect Marcia?"

"I'm with you now, aren't I?"

When they reached Fancy Creek, Melanie got out of the car and slammed the door. She ran off into the woods, leaving him alone. Kaz called after her, but she didn't stop. He lost sight of her in the trees. He wanted to be mad at her game playing, but he could only think about what it would be like to kiss her.

His heart was pounding as he chased her. She excited him like no other girl he had ever known. He started into the trees, trying to find her.

"Melanie!"

Shadows grew darker around him as he moved deeper into the forest. He considered giving up and leaving her alone. Something rustled to his left. He turned toward the noise. Someone jumped at him from behind a tree. Kaz saw the flash of golden hair.

Melanie grabbed him, almost knocking him to

the ground. He was startled. Then he felt her lips on his face. She kissed him all over. Kaz tried to take her into his arms, but she broke away, fleeing once again through the trees.

"Melanie, get back here!"

He could hear the echo of her laughter. Her teasing was beginning to annoy him, but he was determined to play along. The payoff, he was sure, would be worth it.

"I'm going to leave you!" he cried.

"Over here, Kaz."

The voice had caught him unawares. He went in the direction of her voice. When he found her, Melanie had spread out a tablecloth in a clearing. She had also set up their picnic lunch.

He was hooked. She was like a sugar treat. The more he tasted, the more he wanted. He had never known a girl like her.

"I don't know what I'm going to do with you, Melanie."

She sat down on the tablecloth, glancing up at him with half-opened eyes. "I'm sure you'll think of something."

A shaft of sunlight spilled through the leaves, bouncing off her golden hair. She looked up at him and smiled. He admired her perfect neck and her flawless complexion and the fringe of hair around her beautifully shaped ear.

"Would you like a sandwich?" she asked.

Kaz shook his head. "No, I'm not hungry."

Melanie patted the cloth next to her. "Neither am I."

Kaz sat down beside her. Their lips came together immediately. He wrapped his arms around her. It was a long time before they finally ate their picnic lunch.

Marcia's hand trembled as she picked up the phone. She quickly dialed the number she had gotten from directory assistance. Her heart pounded as she waited for someone to answer. She was taking a big chance, calling out of the blue. But she wasn't ready to give up.

"Hello, Mrs. Kasden? . . . This is Marcia Granholm. I was wondering if Kaz was around—I mean Wayne. . . ." But Wayne wasn't in. He had gone out for the day and Mrs. Kasden didn't know when he would be back. Marcia didn't want to leave a message. But she was embarrassed to think that Mrs. Kasden would tell Kaz that she had called.

When Marcia hung up, she felt stupid, rejected. Why had she called? Because she still liked him? Yes, that was it, and she wanted so desperately for him to like her.

He was probably out with another girl. But it didn't matter. Marcia wasn't ready to give up on him. A boy like Kaz took a lot of time and patience. And Marcia was willing to wait.

# Chapter 5

By the end of his second week in school, Kaz thought he was having the best time of his life. The girls of Cresswell High were keeping him busy, but he had risen to the challenge. It was a balancing act, with Carol, Marcia, Sally, and his beloved Melanie. Because of the juggling routine, Kaz had been forced to invent ways to keep the girls from finding out that he was dating all of them.

He imparted his first rule in a manner consistent with their personalities—no affection in school. Kaz told them that he was a private person. He didn't want anyone to know his business. When he passed the girls in the hall, he would smile and wink. But he never let on to anyone that he was dating one girl, much less four of them.

He even avoided the inevitable lunch date in the cafeteria. He went off campus for the noon meal. It kept them all happy and gave Kaz a sense of mystery. He couldn't have pulled it off any other way.

On Friday afternoon, Kaz sat in his last class, considering his fantastic luck in love. Carol was his weekday girl. He had been to her house three nights in the past week. He put her off for the weekend by saying his parents were taking him out of town. She had bought the lie.

Marcia was on again for that evening. They were going to another foreign film in Porterville. Kaz was looking forward to something more than idle conversation after the movie. Maybe she would invite him inside this time. He could always ask her to help him on his term paper.

Sally was his rock-and-roll woman. They were set for a Sunday afternoon concert in Westbury, a nearby community. At least last weekend's band wasn't on the bill. Sally was going to cook dinner afterward. Kaz couldn't wait.

Then there was Melanie. Saturday was reserved for his blond goddess. They didn't have any concrete plans. Melanie liked to be spontaneous. Kaz was ready to play along. He would do anything to be with her.

The bell rang, freeing him from the confines of academia. He hurried to his car. Walking through the parking lot, he caught a glimpse of Ricky Buller and his gang. They were lurking around the black pickup truck. Kaz had tried to make amends with Ricky, but the bully was still swearing revenge. Kaz had shrugged off the new threats. He had other things on his mind.

On the way home, Kaz stopped to get gas. The oil was low in the Miata, so Kaz let the station mechanic add a quart. While he was waiting, he gazed out toward the street. He was surprised when he saw a familiar blond girl hurrying by across the street.

"Melanie," he said with a wry smile.

She was walking with quick, determined steps, probably off on one of her shoplifting sprees, Kaz imagined. Kaz smiled to himself. He wanted to play a joke on her. After he paid the mechanic, he drove down the street in search of Melanie.

On the second block, he spotted her entering a boutique. Quickly he parked the car and entered the store. She was on the far side of the room, flipping through racks of skirts. Something seemed different about her. She was dressed in a blue-and-white suit. She wore a white silk blouse beneath the suit jacket.

Kaz walked up behind her. "Excuse me, miss. Store security. I'd like to check your purse."

The girl turned slowly, flashing a perturbed expression. "I beg your pardon?"

"What are you snitching now?" he asked, winking.

She frowned. "I think you have me confused with someone else." She turned her back on him.

Kaz laughed nervously. Something was wrong here. "What's with you?"

She turned back, glaring at him. "I think you're looking for my twin sister Melanie."

Kaz's mouth hung open. "What?"

"My sister is the kleptomaniac. Not me."

Kaz wasn't buying the act. "Oh yeah? If you're her twin sister, how come I haven't seen you at Cresswell High?"

"I'm in an accelerated program," she replied impatiently. "I've been away for two weeks in Boston. I'll be back in school on Monday."

The sales clerk stepped up next to them. "Hi, Tiffany. May I help you with something today?"

Kaz grimaced. "Tiffany?"

The clerk glared at him. "Is this young man bothering you?"

Kaz blushed. "No. I was just leaving."

He hurried out of the store, stopping at the first pay phone. He quickly dialed Melanie's number. She picked up on the third ring. Kaz talked to her for a few minutes, making sure she was ready for their date on Saturday. He didn't say anything about her equally gorgeous sister Tiffany.

After he hung up, he grabbed the phone book. There were two listings for Kaylor at different addresses. Their parents were probably separated.

He turned to see Tiffany walking out of the boutique. She was just as beautiful as Melanie, the same hair, an identical face, an exact copy in living color.

Kaz ran after her. "Hey, Tiffany. Wait."

She stopped and looked back with a frown. "What's your problem?"

He gazed into her lovely face. "You're my problem."

Tiffany Kaylor sniffed condescendingly. "If you associate with my sister—"

"No way," Kaz replied. "I can't stand her. I caught her shoplifting at a store where my friend works. She's bad news. I thought you were her. I was going to try to stop you from ripping off that store."

Her expression softened a little. Kaz had told

the lies without even thinking. He wanted Tiffany to like him. He flashed his best smile.

"So, you go to Cresswell?" Tiffany asked.

Kaz nodded. He noticed the look in her eye. She had become aware of his good looks. But she would still be a tough nut to crack. He could tell that she was different from her sister, even if they did look exactly alike.

"May I help with your packages?" he asked.

Tiffany shook her head. "I can handle them."

She started walking again. Kaz fell in beside her. It was eerie.

"Allow me to apologize," Kaz said, switching on the charm.

"For what?"

"Mistaking you for your sister. I can tell you're nothing like her."

Tiffany gave a mocking laugh. "You're very perceptive. Why haven't I seen *you* at Cresswell before?"

"I just started two weeks ago," Kaz replied. "I just moved up from Florida."

"How exciting."

Kaz sighed. "I guess I haven't made a very good impression on you."

"That's an understatement," Tiffany replied.

But Kaz wasn't ready to give up. "What does your father do?"

Before she could reply, a horn honked on the street. A sleek-looking red Porsche pulled up to the curb. A smiling, blondish man waved to Tiffany.

"Why don't you ask him yourself?" Tiffany replied with a smirk. "Here he is now."

The man got out of the car. He was wearing a double-breasted glen plaid sports jacket and wrinkled linen trousers. His broad face was covered by a pair of Italian racing sunglasses.

"Hi, princess," he said to Tiffany.

Kaz fought off his nervousness. Tiffany had seemed too far out of reach. He wanted her. Somehow everything that had come before didn't matter. Now he had to score points with her father.

"Jim Kaylor," he said, extending his hand to Kaz.

Kaz shook hands with him. "Wayne Kasden, sir."

"Sir? Tiff honey, why didn't you tell me that you were dating a gentleman?"

Tiffany grimaced at her father. "Daddy!"

His grin was wide and toothy. He put his hand on Kaz's shoulder. "I came to pick her up, Wayne. She hates to drive, can you believe it? I offered to buy her a car, but she won't hear of it. Hey, I can afford it, too. My video stores are bringing in the buckaloanies."

Kaz squinted at him. "That wouldn't be Video Vibrations, would it?"

"You know my stores!"

"I've only been here a couple of weeks, but I've already been in your store, the one at Pelham Four Corners."

Jim Kaylor nodded approvingly. "That's my flagship. It's bringing in the *dinero*. Say, what's your favorite kind of movie?"

Kaz could feel Tiffany glaring right through

him. "I like the old stuff. You know, classics. John Wayne and James Stewart."

"Tiffany, why haven't you told me about this boy?" Jim Kaylor barked. "She keeps her romances secret, Wayne."

Tiffany started toward the Porsche. "Let's go, Daddy. I still have to unpack from my trip."

"Now hold on, Tiff," her father replied. "Wayne, what are you doing for dinner tonight?"

Tiffany directed her narrow eyes on her father. "Daddy!"

Kaz shrugged. "Well, sir, I—"

"You're coming to dinner at my place," Jim Kaylor went on.

"Daddy!"

Kaz looked at the ground, giving his bashful act a try. "I wouldn't dream of putting Tiffany on the spot, sir."

He looked back at his daughter. "Tiffany, I think you should spend some time with this young man. Get your head out of those books."

"Daddy, I have to study."

"No, you don't. Not tonight. It's Friday."

Kaz smiled at Jim Kaylor. "Sir, I—"

"I won't take no for an answer, Wayne. Here, let me give you our address in Gaspee Farms."

He took a card from his shirt pocket, writing down the address and phone number. When he handed the card to Kaz, he saw that it was a coupon for a free video rental. Jim Kaylor winked and told him to be on time.

"Thank you," Kaz said. "Thanks a lot, Mr. Kaylor."

"Call me Jimbo!"

He turned to walk back toward the Porsche. Tiffany also got into the car. As they drove off, she shot a hostile look at Kaz. But he didn't care. He had to take his shot. But there was a phone call to make. He ran to the pay phone.

"Hello, Marcia. . . . Yeah, it's me, Kaz. Listen, something has come up. . . ."

When Marcia hung up the phone, she fought the urge to cry. It hurt deeply to have Kaz break their date. She knew he was seeing someone else. She could feel it. He wasn't a one girl type of guy. Still, she had been so excited when he had finally called again.

Marcia sat on the edge of her bed, looking at her schoolbooks. She was so good at scholastics and so bad at everything else. Why couldn't she pick a guy who was good for her? She always went for the hunks with no manners, no depth. Maybe she should wise up and go out with someone who was less attractive than Kaz.

She tossed her books aside. She couldn't bring herself to study. After all, it was Friday night. Everyone else was having a good time. Marcia wanted to have some fun, too. Why should she sit home in a weepy mood?

The phone rang again a few minutes later. Marcia didn't answer her extension. It couldn't be for her. But a moment later, her father called up the stairs and told her to pick up.

"Hello?"

"Hi, doll. It's me, Ricky."

She sighed. Just what she needed to make her feel worse. Ricky was such an oaf. The worst mistake she had ever made.

"Ricky, I thought I told you to leave me alone."

"I can't get you out of my mind, babe. What do you say we get together tonight?"

She hung up. Tears welled in her eyes. She thought about Kaz again. There was something there. She knew it. But he wouldn't see things her way. Marcia wanted to take it slow. She didn't want to rush into a physical relationship. There was too much room for trouble.

But Kaz was too fast for her. Maybe she should give up on him. But when she thought about his handsome face and his charming manners, she decided to keep hoping.

"I told you he was good-looking, Dana."

A pretty young woman, Jim Kaylor's date, had joined them for dinner at the house in Gaspee Farms. Mr. Kaylor had brought in Chinese food in white cartons. He had been drinking wine through dinner, which made him somewhat tipsy.

He grinned at Kaz. "You play any ball, Wayne?"

Kaz shrugged. "No, but I'd like to. Unfortunately we move around too much."

"Your old man with the power company?"

"Yes, sir."

Tiffany sat at the table with her arms folded. She hadn't spoken more than five words throughout dinner. Kaz was playing it cool. He was polite to Tiffany, but he was careful not to appear too eager. And it was strange, sitting at the same table with her. She looked like Melanie, but she was much more reserved and refined. Somehow her father's vulgar nature hadn't rubbed off on her.

Mr. Kaylor turned his wineglass upside down. "Empty!" he proclaimed.

Kaz smiled, even though Mr. Kaylor's drinking made him uncomfortable.

Mr. Kaylor got up and headed to the wine cabinet. As he passed his date, he bent and gave her a peck on the cheek. The auburn-haired girl was not much older than Tiffany.

"You want some more wine, Dana?" Mr. Kaylor asked.

His girl smiled. "Anything you say, Jimbo."

Kaz glanced at Tiffany, who was stone-faced. He knew how mortified she must be to have anyone know about her gauche, bullying father. Kaz decided that the only way to earn her appreciation would be to go home and save her from further embarrassment. He got his opportunity a moment later.

"How about coffee?" Mr. Kaylor asked Kaz.

"No, thank you, sir. It keeps me up at night. In fact, if you'll excuse me, I have to go home and help my folks with some things."

Kaz bid them all farewell, and in a few minutes he stepped out the front door into the sweet night air.

Then the door opened behind him, and Tiffany hurried down the path.

"Help your folks," she said mockingly. "That's some story on a Friday night." Then she gave him a big, warm smile and started laughing.

"Was it that obvious?" Kaz asked.

"It was to me. Who cares what they think," said Tiffany. "Now maybe you should think of a good excuse to be with me. Do you think you can?" She looked at him slyly.

Kaz was ready to let out a cheer. He could barely contain himself. "Well, I could use some help with my term paper," he said.

"All right, I'll help," she said eagerly.

"We could ride over to my place," Kaz suggested calmly.

"All right."

Kaz led her to the Miata. When she sat beside him, Kaz felt the incredible energy of his attraction. She was deeper, more substantive than Melanie. He wanted to know what was going on inside her head. She didn't wait long to tell him.

"I can't stand it when he brings them home," she offered glumly. "They're always younger than he is. Did you see how she flirted with you?"

"I didn't notice. I was too busy watching you."

"I see," she said.

"What about your mother?" Kaz asked, even though he already knew.

"She's worse," Tiffany replied. "My sister lives with her. I don't get along with either one of them."

"I'm sorry," he said sincerely.

"No. I'm the one who should be sorry. I've been horrible to you."

He smiled warmly. "It's not your fault. You're an intelligent and sensitive girl. And you seem—I don't know—lonely. You deserve better."

She looked at him. "I misjudged you."

"Forget it," he said, looking at the road.

She touched his arm. "You're nice. Let's go out to Indian Point."

"Sure," he said. It sounded romantic.

She seemed to relax as she gave him directions. They went for a romantic walk along the cliffs, near Lighthouse Bay. But Kaz played it cool. He didn't want to scare her off.

At the end of the evening, when he took her home, he wasn't going to try for a good-night kiss. But then she put her soft hand on his cheek. She told him she had enjoyed their time together.

Kaz put his arms around her. Their lips touched lightly. Her kiss transported him to a place he had never been before. When they broke off, he was light-headed.

"Tiffany—"

"Yes?"

Kaz sighed. He could not tell her how much he needed her. That would come later, after all the trouble began.

Marcia got tired of sitting in her room, so she decided to take a bike ride through Cresswell. It was a warm night, and she knew she would be safe if she stayed in the well-lit neighborhoods. She guided her three-speed racer down Washington Street, heading for the winding byways of Gaspee Farms.

Her spirits lifted a little as she worked off some of her sorrows. Her legs pumped hard on the inclines. The wind rushed over her as the bike swept downhill.

Marcia grabbed the handbrakes when she saw the car. It had to belong to Kaz. What other red Miata, parked in Gaspee Farms, would have Florida license plates?

Marcia climbed off the bike and peered toward the front porch of the house. Her heart skipped a beat when she saw Kaz kissing the blond girl. It was Tiffany Kaylor, Melanie's twin sister.

"No!"

Marcia turned away with tears in her eyes. He had broken their date to go out with someone else. She got on her bike again, riding away from the spectacle that broke her heart. She knew she had to forget about Kaz. But somehow the image of his handsome face stayed fresh in her thoughts.

Kaz haunted her, even in her sleep. She dreamed horrible nightmares about him that night. She awoke in a sweat, wishing that she had never met him.

# Chapter 6

"Are you all right?" Melanie asked.

Kaz nodded absently. "Sure, why?"

"You seem distracted," she replied.

Kaz sighed. "I'm a little tired."

They were in the Miata, on their way to the park. Kaz was still thinking about the previous evening, when he had kissed Tiffany good night. Melanie's twin sister had gotten to him.

"Pull over at the next intersection," Melanie said. "I need to get some things."

Kaz guided the car into the parking lot of a drugstore. "Can you get what you need here?"

"Sure," Melanie replied. "It's one of those chain stores. They have it all."

As soon as they entered the store, Melanie went into her act. She picked up a canvas beach bag and began to stuff it with soaps, shampoos, and a box of candy. Kaz felt the rush of adrenaline as he walked behind her. She seemed indiscriminate about what she was stealing. It worried him. She was getting too reckless for her own good.

"Melanie, are you—?"

"Shh, chill out."

They were heading for the front door when the

store manager stepped from behind the shelves to grab Melanie's arm. "Just one minute, young lady."

Melanie shrugged away from him. "Get your hands off me."

Kaz stepped between them. "What's the problem?"

"Shoplifting," the manager said.

"No way!" Melanie replied. "We were going to pay for this."

"Tell it to the sheriff."

Melanie turned to Kaz with a pleading expression on her face.

Kaz acted indignant. "Hold it right there. We weren't stealing anything."

The store manager pointed to Melanie's bag. "What do you call that?"

"We didn't want to use your plastic bags," Kaz replied quickly. "Or haven't you heard of the environmental movement?"

The store manager frowned. "You were heading for the door."

"Yes," Kaz said. "She was going to wait for me while I went to get my wallet. I left it in the car. Besides, even if we were stealing—which we weren't—it's not shoplifting until we're outside."

The man stepped back, knowing that Kaz was technically correct.

Melanie smirked at him. "Still want to call the sheriff?"

The store manager scowled in his defeat. "All right, smart guy. Go get your wallet. Then you can come back here to pay for the stuff. After that, I never want to see you in my store again."

"Thanks," Kaz said with a wry smile.

Back on the highway, Melanie was all over him. Her arms were around his waist. She kissed his face and neck.

"Did you see his expression?" Melanie said. "You really got him."

Kaz nodded, not feeling the same enthusiasm. They had almost gotten caught. He could just see his father bailing him out.

"Hey, Kaz. Have I told you lately that I love you?"

"No," he said, catching his breath.

Melanie pursed her lips in a mock kiss. "You're irresistible. You've got it all."

Kaz felt a strange gnawing in the pit of his stomach. For the first time since he had been dating all the girls, Kaz was confused. He hadn't been prepared for Melanie and Tiffany. They were the flip sides of the same record, yin and yang, heads and tails of the coin.

"Do you love me?" Melanie asked, grinning mischievously.

Kaz gave her a sideways glance. "Of course I love you."

"What do you mean 'of course'?"

"I mean you should know I love you."

Melanie pursed her lips. "Then prove it."

They continued on to the park. The place was crowded with picnickers and Frisbee throwers since it was a bright, Saturday afternoon. Melanie said she knew a secluded spot. She led him down a path to a grove of trees near a brook.

Kaz started to spread out the beach blanket. He was still in an addled mood. His nerves were tingling from the incident in the drugstore. He was also thinking about Tiffany.

"Hey, over here!"

He turned to look at Melanie. She had doffed her shirt and shorts. Her slender frame was covered by a green, Day-Glo string bikini. She turned for him like a fashion model.

"What do you think, my handsome love-puppy?"

The tightness spread through his chest. He couldn't find the words. Melanie had cast her spell again. For the moment, he stopped thinking about Tiffany.

When Kaz got back from the park, he checked the messages on his answering machine.

Sally's voice was first. "Hi, honey. I'm at work. I'm ready for the concert tomorrow. I'm also ready for you. I miss you, babe. Stay in touch."

He sighed. "Sure."

The next message was from someone who hung up without saying a word. Maybe it was Marcia. Or Tiffany. Tiffany was on his mind.

A third message was from Carol. "Kaz, you dirtbag. I'm mad at you. Not really. I just miss you. My mom's going out tonight. Want to come over when you get home? You have my number."

He leaned back on his bed, exhaling. "This isn't going to be as easy as I thought."

The phone rang again. Kaz held his breath. He waited for the machine to click on so he could monitor the call.

"Hi there, partner in crime. Are you home yet?"

Kaz hesitated. Something inside would not let him answer Melanie's call. He just kept listening.

"Okay, babe. You better not be out with another girl. I'll kill you if you are. Just kidding. I'd only maim you. I just wanted to tell you that I had a great time at the park. Let's do it again tonight, when there's no crowd, after dark. You won't be sorry. Ciao, love-puppy."

Kaz put his hands behind his head, staring at the wall. He was starting to worry about Melanie. She was too unpredictable. And her carelessness had almost gotten them arrested. He wondered what Melanie would do if she found out about the other girls. She would throw a fit, maybe even get nasty.

Kaz jumped when the phone rang again. "Hi, it's Tiffany. I hope you don't—"

He switched off the machine and picked up the receiver. "Hi there."

"Oh, you're home," she said.

"I just walked in. How are you?"

She sighed. "Fine. I had a great time last night."

"So did I."

He felt warm inside. Her voice was softer. It lacked the edge of Melanie's tone. She was good and pure, not like her delinquent sister.

"Are you busy?" she asked tentatively.

"I don't know. Why?"

"Daddy wants me to go with him to Shell Island tonight, and he said I could invite you," she went on. "We have a house there. We'll stay tonight and come back tomorrow."

"I don't know, Tiffany."

His heart was pounding.

"It's a big house," she replied. "You'll have your own room. It's nice. We can walk on the beach. Don't worry, you won't have to socialize with Daddy."

He couldn't say no. She needed him. He could hear the longing in her sweet voice.

"I'll have to clear it with my mom and dad," Kaz replied.

*And make excuses to Melanie and Sally.*

"Then you'll go?" Tiffany asked.

"I wouldn't miss it for the world," he said, wondering what Tiffany looked like in a bathing suit.

"I'll split gas with you," Tiffany went on. "And the fee for the ferry. It's almost thirty dollars if we take your car."

"That sounds fine with me."

"Anything to get away from Dad and Dana," she said with a groan. "If we work it right, we won't even have to see them."

"I'll pick you up at six," Kaz said.

"Love it. See you then."

"I can't wait."

"Kaz?"

"Yeah?"

"You're the best. Thanks. See you."

They hung up. Kaz took a deep breath. Sally and Melanie weren't going to like his breaking off their dates. But Kaz didn't care. He was going to be with Tiffany. Suddenly that was all that mattered.

# Chapter 7

Kaz saw Tiffany's blond hair coming toward him on the beach. She had her arms outstretched. He ran toward her, but when he was close enough to see her face, Tiffany was no longer there. Instead, the slender body had sprouted four heads that belonged to Carol, Marcia, Melanie, and Sally.

The four girls began to scream at him. He heard Tiffany's voice chiding him for his infidelity. Claws came up, ripping his face. Blood poured down his cheeks. He felt sharp teeth in his neck.

Kaz cried out and sat up. Sweat dripped off his face instead of blood. He looked around his room. The dream had seemed so real.

Kaz glanced at his clock radio. It was five o'clock in the morning. He had gotten back late the night before from Shell Island. He had enjoyed the jaunt with Tiffany, even though she had spent a great deal of their time together complaining about her father and his younger girlfriend. But there had also been romantic walks on the beach, complete with hugging and kissing, the things that made them forget their troubles.

Climbing out of bed, Kaz switched on a light over his desk. He opened a desk drawer, taking out a stack of photographs. Carol, Marcia, Melanie, and Sally had given him pictures of themselves. The fifth picture was of Tiffany, taken last summer by a strolling photographer on Shell Island. He treasured the photograph of Tiffany more than any of the others.

He spread the pictures on his bed. Tiffany's pretty face jumped out at him. She looked like Melanie, but the difference was obvious. If they were standing side by side, he would have been able to tell the difference. Tiffany was the good girl. Melanie was the bad girl.

Kaz wiped the sweat from his forehead. Something had to change. No matter how hard he tried, he would not be able to keep up with all of them. He could drop everyone but the twins. He had to have them. The others could go, but it would have to be quick, painless.

He leaned back on the bed, closing his eyes. Who would he tell first? He fell asleep again before he could make a decision. The next thing he heard was his mother calling him to breakfast.

"I love you, Marcia."

"No, Kaz. Please."

"Listen to me, Marcia."

She turned away from him. "No, Kaz. It won't work. We're just too different. It would never work."

"We can make it work, Marcia. I know we can."

She wheeled back toward him, looking into his handsome face. "Oh, Kaz . . ."

"We'll get to know each other, Marcia. I can wait

69

as long as you want me to. It doesn't matter, just as long as I'm with you."

"Kaz—I—I love you, but what about Tiffany Kaylor?"

"Who?"

"Kiss me, Kaz."

She bent her head back. His lips were coming toward hers. She anticipated the electric feeling of their touch.

"Marcia, honey?"

Suddenly Kaz was gone. Marcia heard a rude banging. She opened her eyes and sat up in her bed. Her father was calling her from the hall.

"Marcia, you must've forgotten to set your alarm again. It's seven o'clock. You don't want to be late for school."

It had been a dream. The same dream that had come every night since she had seen Kaz kissing Tiffany Kaylor. Marcia was still hung up on Kaz. But there was nothing she could do, save climb out of bed and face the dreariness of the day.


Kaz strode anxiously toward the front door of Cresswell High. He took the concrete steps two at a time. When he entered the hall, he turned away from the office. He didn't want to run into Marcia.

As he headed toward homeroom, he saw Carol coming toward him.

Kaz tried to smile. "Hi, Carol. You're just the person I wanted to—"

Carol slapped his face. "You rat!"

Kaz touched the stinging flesh. "Carol, what—?"

"I hate you, Wayne Kasden!"

Her voice was loud enough to stop several people in the hall. A small crowd began to grow. Everyone liked to watch a fight.

"What did I do?" Kaz asked in a penitent tone.

Carol pushed him. "I heard about you!"

"What?"

"You jerk!"

"Carol—"

"Saturday," Carol said. "Friends of mine were at the park. They saw you and your blond bimbo frolicking. How could you cheat on me like that?"

Kaz tried to take her arm. "Carol, please—"

She shrugged away, continuing to rant at him. Kaz broke a sweat. He had to shut her up before the whole school found out. He didn't want Tiffany to hear about their argument.

"I thought we had something special," Carol said. "Those evenings at my house. Didn't they mean anything to you?"

Kaz shook his head. "You've got it all wrong, Carol. It's not like that. I swear."

"What about the blonde? Huh?"

"Carol, she's my cousin," Kaz lied. "I had to take her to the park. My mother made me."

"What?"

Kaz tried to smile again. "Listen, let's talk tonight, okay? I'll come over about eight. We can straighten this whole thing out then."

"You better, Kaz. I mean it. Nobody cheats on me and gets away with it. You hear me?"

"Everybody hears you."

Carol stormed away.

71

Kaz turned to see a blond head of hair bobbing away from the crowd.

"Melanie!" he muttered under his breath.

He took flight for his homeroom. When he came through the door, he saw Melanie sitting at her desk. He tried to study her expression, wondering if she had heard him arguing with Carol.

She looked in his direction, frowning. When Kaz smiled, she turned away. *What had she heard?* he wondered. What kind of elaborate fabrication would he have to create about canceling their date on Saturday night?

When the crowd had gathered in the hallway, Marcia had come out of the office to see what the commotion was about. Her eyes had opened wide at the sight of Kaz arguing with Carol. Apparently, Tiffany Kaylor was not his only other love interest at Cresswell.

After the argument had broken off, Marcia went back to the office, taking her place behind the desk. Somehow, she felt superior to Kaz. But she didn't feel any better about the fact that she wasn't seeing him. He seemed to have forgotten about her.

Marcia sighed. Her heart was nursing the slightest ember of the spark that would not die. She saw herself straightening out the beautiful boy with the slick manner. Marcia would get him to see the light, that girls meant more than good-night kisses and loose moments. Love could be real. Love could change a person, make a difference in that person's life.

But how would she get together with him? She had no way of knowing that fate would toss them together in the darkest of circumstances. Marcia simply went back to her morning tasks, trying not to think about Kaz's steel-blue eyes.

Kaz spent the rest of the school day avoiding the girls. He didn't flirt with Sally in English class. Melanie was cold anyway, so there was no problem getting around her. Marcia was not even in his thoughts. And Tiffany was in her special program, so they rarely crossed paths in school.

The only person he managed to see was Ricky Buller, whose arm had come out of the sling. He glared at Kaz in the senior parking lot. Kaz ignored him. He wanted to get home. He had to figure out his strategy for dumping Carol.

When he got home, the pictures of the girls were still on the bed in his room. He picked up Carol's photograph.

"Punky little Carol."

He had to break it off. He tore the picture in half. The pieces fluttered into his wastebasket.

"It's over, babe. I've got to do it."

But by the time eight o'clock rolled around, he still was not sure about what he would say to Carol.

# Chapter 8

Carol's house was nearly dark when Kaz pulled the Miata into the parking space out front. A single light burned on the second story. Her mother was probably working. As Kaz got out of the car, he could see shadows moving on the wall in the upstairs bedroom. Carol was home. He wanted to get it over with.

He took a deep breath and moved up the walk. His stomach churned as he clomped up the front steps. For all his calculated cool, Kaz was still nervous about breaking off with Carol. What if she decided to make things tough for him?

He was about to knock on the front door when he realized that it was already half-open. Something wasn't right. Kaz pushed through the doorway. He called, but Carol didn't reply.

Kaz heard a noise upstairs. He hoped she wasn't planning some lovelorn scene. He wanted it to be finished quickly, no tears, no emotion. It just hadn't worked out, plain and simple.

"Carol?"

The house was suddenly quiet. The tightness spread through his whole body. What if she wanted to hurt him? She had a horrible temper.

"Carol?"

There was no sound. He started to climb the stairs to her room, where he had once had so much fun. He moved carefully along the dark hallway. He saw the light spilling through the crack in her door.

"Carol? It's me, Kaz."

Dead silence.

"Carol, come on."

He was starting to grow angry with her. He didn't like playing games unless he was the one who made the rules. He went toward the light and pushed open the door.

Her body was on the bed. Her face was pale. Her lips had turned blue, and her tongue lolled out of her mouth. A pair of black mesh stockings had been wrapped around her neck. Kaz knew immediately that she was no longer alive.

"Carol!"

He bent over the bed. She had been strangled with her own stockings. He touched her wrist—no pulse.

"Carol! No, don't let her be dead."

Sweat broke on his face. His body began to tremble. Could he revive her? How long had she been dead? Her body was cold and blue. Her windpipe had been crushed.

Kaz remembered the shadows on the wall. Someone had been in the room a few moments before he arrived. He glanced toward the open window. Apparently the killer had escaped through the window as Kaz was walking into the house.

Rushing to the window, he peered into the darkness of the alley below. The Upper Basin was bathed in a shroud of shadows. The neighborhood was quiet. The killer had already escaped through the alleyway.

As he turned away from the window, Kaz caught a glimpse of the mirror on Carol's dresser. He stopped cold. Someone had written a message in lipstick.

DATE THIS, LOVER BOY.

Kaz almost dropped to the floor. Someone had known he was coming. The killer was trying to frame him. The police were probably on the way. He would be caught red-handed. He had to get out of there.

He stopped himself. "No, not yet."

He had to get rid of any evidence that would link him to Carol. He grabbed a handful of tissues from her dresser, wiping the lipstick message from the mirror. He slipped the tissues into his pants pocket.

He looked around the room. His picture was in a frame on the nightstand next to Carol's bed. Using tissues to mask his fingerprints, he removed the picture from the frame. Then he put the frame in the closet, under some boxes on a shelf. Frantically, he searched for more evidence of their relationship. If he could just get out, he would be free from the horror. He hadn't killed Carol. Why should he pay for her murder?

He stole one last look at her body. Tears pooled in his eyes. In his own way he had loved her. But that didn't matter now. He had to bolt.

Kaz ran out, tearing down the stairs. He flew toward his car, praying that no one had seen him come and go. It was a dark neighborhood. Maybe he had gotten away without anyone noticing him.

He put the car in gear and started home.

"Carol. Somebody killed Carol."

He felt lost and horrified as he drove back to Rocky Bank Estates. They were going to suspect him for sure. Everyone had seen them fighting in the hall. He couldn't deny it. But he hadn't killed her. No one could prove a thing. He was not going to fry for a murder he didn't commit.

When he got back to the house, there was no one home. His parents were out for the evening. He went upstairs and immediately flushed the soiled tissue down the toilet. He also tore up his picture and flushed it down the toilet along with the tissue.

Kaz felt a chill when he saw the lipstick on his pants pocket. He went down to the basement, putting his pants in the washing machine. He had to get rid of all traces of the lipstick. No one was going to pin her murder on him.

"Carol."

He went back to his room. He had never been in such a predicament before. Maybe he should come clean and go to the sheriff. After all, he hadn't killed her.

But they would blame him for her death. The sheriff might lock him up. His family would be disgraced for something he didn't do. Even if there was no evidence against him, someone would fabricate some. Someone would come forward and say they had seen him coming out of the house. Maybe someone had seen the real murderer. But he couldn't count on that.

Who had killed her? Someone they both knew? Ricky Buller! He had sworn revenge against Kaz. But why would he kill Carol? He would be more likely to kill Marcia.

Kaz almost jumped out of his skin when the phone rang. He waited for the machine to answer the call. It was Tiffany.

"Hi," he said breathlessly.

"What's wrong?" she asked. "You sound funny."

"I just ran up the stairs. I was in the basement. I've been here all evening, doing my homework."

He hoped she bought the lie. She could repeat it to the sheriff if he needed an alibi.

"I just wanted to say hi," she told him. "I miss you."

He sighed deeply. "I miss you, too. It's good to hear your voice."

"Kaz, are you all right?"

*No, I found a dead body tonight!*

"Yeah, it's just this darned term paper. I've been at it all night."

"I can always help you," she offered.

"Maybe later on this week," he said. He wasn't in the mood to see anyone now. His hands were trembling so badly that he could barely hold on to the phone. He listened to her as she went on about trivial matters. Finally they said good night and hung up.

Kaz knew he wouldn't be able to sleep all night. He still had to be ready for school the next day. He had to get his act down. He wanted to be casual, in case someone asked him about the dead girl whose blue body lay draped across a bed in the Upper Basin.

# Chapter 9

"Wayne Kasden, please report to the assistant principal's office."

Kaz looked up at the loudspeaker. He had been sitting in history class, anticipating the dull thud of the dropping bomb. Now he had to get through it without losing his cool.

As he got up, he glanced toward Melanie. A tight, sly smirk had turned her mouth into a thin line. Her eyes glistened in the yellow, incandescent light. Kaz turned away from her and went into the hallway.

There had been no reports of Carol's death, not yet anyway. Kaz had listened to the radio all night. He had also tuned in the morning news programs. But word of her murder had not yet reached the media.

Mr. Lipton was waiting for him when he came into the office. "Sit down, Mr. Kasden."

Kaz hurried into the office and sat down next to a man in a gray police uniform. He didn't force a smile. He figured that anyone who had been called to the assistant principal's office should be nervous.

The man in the gray uniform shifted in his seat. He was a big, ruddy man. He looked at Kaz as if he were already tried and convicted. Kaz was afraid of him and tried to stave off the fear and agony that gnawed into his guts.

Mr. Lipton focused his hawk eyes on Kaz. "This is Sheriff Hagen, Mr. Kasden. He wants to talk to you."

Kaz turned to look the sheriff directly in the eye. He tried to look baffled, as if he had absolutely no idea why a police officer should want to speak to him.

Sheriff Hagen's eyes narrowed. "Wayne, do you know a girl named Carol Ledbetter?"

"Yes, sir. I helped her fix her scooter once. She's a friend of mine."

Sheriff Hagen paused, as if he was waiting for Kaz to add something. But Kaz held steady. He felt a bead of sweat trickling down his face.

"Are you nervous?" the sheriff asked.

Kaz tried to laugh. "Yes, sir. I'm always nervous when I get called to Mr. Lipton's office."

"You get in trouble a lot, Wayne?" the sheriff asked blankly.

"No, sir," Kaz replied firmly, looking at Mr. Lipton for confirmation. He was sure that something so incidental as an altercation in the parking lot wouldn't be brought up now.

"He got into a fight," Mr. Lipton said, dashing any hope that Kaz had that Mr. Lipton would make this ordeal easier. "I told you about it, Sheriff. The other boy started it. Ricky Buller."

"Did you hurt him?" the sheriff asked, staring at Kaz with his puffy, cynical eyes.

Kaz sighed. "I dislocated his shoulder. But I'm

81

not proud of it, sir. He came after me, so I defended myself."

"You lost control?"

Kaz felt himself becoming irritated. "No, I didn't."

"You kicked another boy in the groin," the sheriff went on. "You've had some martial arts training, haven't you?"

"There were six of them," Kaz replied a little too testily. "Ask Carol. She was there. She saw the whole thing!"

It had slipped out, but it was a brilliant tactical move. Kaz was proud of himself. He knew the statement would avert suspicion. He had let them know he thought Carol was alive. Now he had to stand firm. He couldn't let them trick him into revealing that he knew she was dead.

"Simmer down," the sheriff said. "You've got a temper."

Kaz took a deep breath, trying to regain his composure. "I'm sorry, sir. It's just that . . . well, I've tried to square things with Ricky, but he keeps making trouble for me. He's the one who's holding the grudge, not me." He had to be careful. He was talking too much now.

Sheriff Hagen turned to the assistant principal. "That true, Mr. Lipton?"

"I've had trouble with Buller before. He seems to have it in for Kasden. From what I was able to glean from the whole thing, Kasden was only defending himself. And he did try to shake hands with Buller. I told them to stay away from each other."

Sheriff Hagen nodded and once again affixed his gaze on Kaz. "This isn't about Ricky Buller. It's about your girlfriend, Carol."

"She's not my girlfriend," Kaz replied. "She's just a friend. What's this all about?"

"I ask the questions. You answer. Understand? Have you ever been to her house before?"

Kaz knew he had to stick close to the truth. His fingerprints would be found in her house. "Yes, sir."

"What did you do there?"

He shrugged. "Watched television, did homework."

The sheriff rubbed his chin. "You had a fight with her in the hall yesterday. Didn't you?"

Kaz frowned. "A fight?"

"I wasn't there," the sheriff said. "Tell me what happened."

Kaz gaped at Hagen. "What's wrong? Why are you asking me all these questions?" He knew he was being led into a trap.

"What makes you think something's wrong?"

"Listen," Kaz replied, "Carol is my friend. If she's in some kind of trouble—"

Hagen frowned. "What makes you think she's in trouble?"

Kaz leaned forward. "Why else would you be here asking me these questions? Look, I want to help her if she's—"

"She's dead," Hagen said quickly. "And I have at least ten witnesses that can say you had a fight with her in the hall yesterday."

Kaz gaped at the sheriff. "Dead? No way!"

Hagen handed him an eight-by-ten color picture of Carol Ledbetter. She was on her bed with the black stocking around her throat. Her face was blue, just as it had been the night before. Kaz dropped the picture. His hands were trembling.

"No!" he cried. "No! Who did this to her?"

"That's what we're here to find out," Mr. Lipton chimed in. "Wayne, what was going on between you and the girl? Be honest."

"We're—we were just friends. I helped her with her scooter. We studied together. That was all."

"What did you fight about in the hall?" the sheriff asked.

Kaz looked straight at the ruddy face, figuring that the truth would keep him out of jail. "It was more like a misunderstanding, sir. One of Carol's friends saw me with another girl. I think Carol wanted to get serious. She wanted to be my girlfriend, but I already have someone else." He was digging his own grave. He knew it.

"What's her name?" Hagen asked.

*Take your choice. There's Melanie, and there's Tiffany, and Sally, and let's not forget Marcia.* "Tiffany Kaylor," he said, and immediately he knew he had made a mistake. It wouldn't be long before they figured out that Carol's friends saw him with *Melanie.*

"You know her, Lipton?"

The assistant principal nodded. "She's a good kid. In the accelerated program. Her father owns a couple of video stores."

Hagen sighed. "Did you go over to Carol's house last night?"

This was the one he was waiting for. He prayed that no one had seen his car in the neighborhood. "No, sir."

"Where were you around eight o'clock?"

"Home."

"Can anyone substantiate that?"

Kaz exhaled. "My parents went out about seven. I was in my room studying all night. Tiffany called me about eight or nine. I don't remember exactly."

"We can check on that," the sheriff offered.

"I hope you do," Kaz replied.

He kept his mouth shut, waiting for the sheriff to accuse him of killing Carol. He worried that he had left something behind in her room, some piece of incriminating evidence. Someone had seen his car on the dark street. He was going to jail.

The bell rang for the end of the period.

Sheriff Hagen exhaled. "Okay, Wayne. You can go."

"What?"

"You can go. Unless you have something else to tell me."

Kaz was relieved. "I don't know what else to tell you. I can't believe anyone could do this."

"Call my office if you think of anything," the sheriff said, looking away dismissively.

Kaz knew the sheriff had more evidence up his sleeve. He had to be careful. He got up, nodded to Mr. Lipton, and headed for the door.

"Kasden?"

He turned to look at Mr. Lipton. "Yes, sir?"

Mr. Lipton focused his hawk eyes on the sheriff.

"For what it's worth, Hagen, I want to go on the record as saying that Wayne is a good kid. He hasn't started any trouble, even if he did finish it with Buller."

"So noted," Hagen replied, still looking away and rubbing his knees with the palms of his hands. "Wayne, keep quiet about this until you hear about it on the news. Is that clear?"

"Yes, sir."

He walked out of the office, moving into the hallway. He had to keep himself together enough to get through the day. He hesitated for a moment, wondering if he should tell the sheriff the whole truth.

But what would it help? No one had seen him coming and going at Carol's place. And even if he had come close to seeing the murderer, he still didn't have a description of the culprit.

He started down the hall again. It was best to keep his mouth shut. There was no sense putting himself into the fire.

"Kaz?"

He jumped when he felt a hand on his shoulder. He turned to see Sally's green eyes staring at him. He started to smile.

"You jerk," Sally said. "It's all over school about you and that blonde you've been seeing."

"Sally—"

"Forget it, Kaz. We're finished."

"But—"

Before he could say another word, Sally turned and stormed away. He had to keep walking. The tardy bell would ring soon. As he headed for the classroom, he passed Melanie in the hallway. She didn't even look at him.

Kaz was flustered. He couldn't concentrate in his next class. He couldn't think of anything but the blue-faced girl with the stocking around her neck.

Kaz drifted like a zombie through the rest of the day, stunned and silent. He was careful to avoid all of his girlfriends.

When the final bell rang, he hurried toward his car. He wanted to get home. He felt like he could sleep for a little while. His body was aching.

As he dropped into the driver's seat of the Miata, he caught a flash of black gliding in front of him. He looked up to see Ricky Buller glaring in his direction. The no-necked jock had a stupid grin on his face. Kaz could still hear his threats on the wind.

*I'm not finished with you, pretty boy.*

The black truck rolled out of the senior parking lot. Kaz wondered if Ricky had known Carol. Maybe he was also from the Upper Basin.

Kaz had to get home. He would conduct his own investigation into Carol's death. If he could find the killer, he could end his own misery.

Marcia heard the news about Sally calling Kaz a jerk in the hallway. He'd been seeing her as well as Carol and Tiffany Kaylor. It only made her feel sorry for him. He wasn't a bad guy, just misguided. The facts could not alter her love for him.

Marcia knew she could change Kaz if she got the

chance. But she was not going to crawl. Despite her feelings for him, Kaz would have to come to her.

She fantasized about how he would beg her to love him. She thought of all the ways he could come back to her. He would repent his sins and beg for her love, which was the only thing that could reform him. But never in her wildest dreams would she have conceived of the path he would soon take to her door.

# Chapter 10

Kaz saw the blue-faced body lying on the bed. He stared at her, reaching out to help. Suddenly, Carol began to rise. She sat up and threw her legs off the bed. Her cold, dead eyes leered back at him.

"You!" she cried. "You did this!"

"No," Kaz said, fumbling for words. "No!"

She began to walk toward him, arms outstretched. "You!"

"No, please, Carol."

"I'm going to get you! I'm going to tell!"

"No!"

Kaz sat up in bed, waking from the horrible dream. Sweat poured from his body. He was horrified. His room was dark and threatening. He had been asleep for a couple of hours. He leaned back for a moment, trying to catch his breath. How long would the nightmare vision haunt him?

He tried to close his eyes again, but suddenly a creaking noise filled the room. The sound seemed to be part of the nightmare. He looked toward the doorway. A shadow moved in the darkness of early evening. A ghostly figure came gliding toward his bed.

Kaz opened his mouth, but nothing came out. His throat was too dry. He could not scream as the dark form hovered over his bed.

"You're dead, lover boy!"

He recognized the voice immediately. "Melanie!"

"Hi, honey. I'm home."

"Babe—"

Melanie shrieked and began to flail at Kaz with her open hands. She slapped his face and his chest. He raised his arms to fend her off. She would not stop. She wanted to hurt him.

"Lover boy! Who was she! Huh?"

"Melanie, please—"

He rolled off the other side of the bed. Melanie kept coming. She dived over the bed, striking at him with her balled-up fists.

"I thought you were different!" she cried. "But you're a rat just like the rest of them!"

Kaz desperately reached upward, grabbing her wrist.

"Let go of me!" Melanie screeched. "I'm going to kill you. Lover boy! Hotshot lover boy!"

He managed to get to his knees, hanging on for dear life. Melanie struck at him with her free hand. Kaz grabbed her arm, twisting it behind her back. He threw her down on the bed, pinning her with his weight.

Melanie tried to bite him, but she couldn't get her teeth into his arm. "It's all over school, lover boy! You've been two-timing me!"

"What do you care?" Kaz said.

"You're the worst!"

"What about *you?*" Kaz shouted. "You don't care about anyone but yourself! You almost got me arrested for shoplifting. What about that? Huh?"

Melanie struggled, but she could not get away from him. Kaz held her down. He was going to accuse her of other things, but the doorbell rang downstairs.

"Just what I needed," he muttered under his breath. "Did my mother let you in?"

Melanie glared at him.

"Did she let you in?"

"No. I let myself in," she replied fiercely. "There was nobody downstairs."

"Great. Just great. I'm going to let you up, but if you try to hurt me, I'm going to pop you. Do you hear me?"

The doorbell rang again.

Melanie nodded reluctantly.

Kaz climbed off her. "I'm going to answer the door. But you better not cause any trouble."

"You've caused all the trouble, lover boy!"

"Stay here," he told her. "I'm not finished with you!"

He hurried downstairs. The doorbell kept chiming. Kaz almost fainted when he looked through the keyhole. He saw the flash of blond hair.

"Tiffany!"

"Kaz, are you in there?"

He didn't want to open the door, but suddenly his mother was there beside Tiffany, reaching for the knob. Tiffany came into the foyer. She smiled when she saw Kaz.

"Hi!"

His face was pale. "Hi."

As soon as his mother was in the kitchen, Tiffany wrapped her arms around Kaz's neck. He hugged her tightly. She felt warm and comforting. But he could not forget about her sister upstairs.

Tiffany drew back a little. "I was running. I jogged over from Gaspee Farms. I had to see you."

Kaz nodded absently, wondering how he was going to get rid of her.

"Are you all right?" she asked.

"Yes, I was taking a nap. I'm always weird when I wake up from a nap."

Tiffany's face grew serious. "Oh, Kaz. Did you hear about that girl?"

"Girl?"

"Carol Ledbetter," Tiffany replied. "Somebody murdered her. It was on the six o'clock news."

A shiver ran through his shoulders. He had to keep himself together in front of Tiffany. He also had to get her out of the house before she discovered that Melanie was in his room.

She put her hand on his chest. Her presence and her touch eased the pain a little. But he could not forget about his worries even when Tiffany pressed her mouth to his.

Kaz kissed her and then broke away. "What did they say about that girl?"

Tiffany sighed. "Kaz, the sheriff talked to me. He asked if I called you last night about eight. I told him that I had talked to you around that time. Kaz, he said that girl was a friend of yours. Was there anything going on between you and Carol?"

"No. I helped her fix her scooter once, that was

all." The lie made him feel horrible. "I think she had a crush on me. But I could never go out with her, not with you in my life."

"Oh, Kaz. I love you so much."

When she embraced him again, he suddenly felt like the worst heel who had ever lived. He almost told her about the other girls, even Melanie. But he had to get her away from the house before he told her anything.

"Tiff—"

She grimaced. "Not *Tiff*. I hate it when my father calls me that."

"Sorry. Tiffany, why don't I give you a ride home?"

"Sure."

He didn't have his keys, his license, or even his shoes. But he had to get her out of there. He didn't like leaving Melanie in his room, but it was better than being discovered by Tiffany.

He went into the kitchen, grabbing his mother's car keys. "I'm going to take Tiffany home, Mom. I'll be right back."

"Okay, honey."

He wondered if his mother would be all right with Melanie in the house. Maybe he should give her a warning before he left. When he came back into the foyer, he told Tiffany to wait a minute, he had to go to his room.

"Oh, I've never seen your room," Tiffany said. "Can I come up?"

Sweat broke on his forehead. "It's a mess. Come on, we better go."

He ushered her outside, into his mother's car.

On the way to Gaspee Farms, Tiffany talked about her father. He would be going away for a while. He was always leaving on business, abandoning her to the empty house. She asked Kaz if he could spend some time with her while her father was gone. He nodded absently, wishing that he had not left Melanie in his room.

When they reached Tiffany's house, she asked him to come inside. Kaz declined, saying that he had to get back for dinner. Tiffany said she understood. They kissed good night, and she got out of the car.

"Are you all right?" she said through the open window.

He nodded. "Yeah, it was just weird hearing about Carol Ledbetter. You be careful, Tiffany."

"I will. I love you. 'Night."

He watched her intently until she was inside the house.

Suddenly Melanie's hostile phone message rang in his ears.

*You better not be out with another girl. I'll kill you if you are.*

He put the car in gear and raced back toward Rocky Bank Estates.


Kaz was worried about Melanie. What if she found the photos of the other girls, or said something to upset his mother?

Kaz rushed into the house. "Mom?"

There was no immediate reply.

"Mom!"

Something bumped in the kitchen. Kaz ran

through the living room. He burst into the kitchen to see his mother lying on her stomach.

"Mom!"

He reached to pick her up.

His mother turned over, looking up at him. "Hi, honey."

"Mom! You scared me to death!"

"I was just trying to fish my ring out from under the stove. I dropped it, and it rolled under there."

Kaz stood up, exhaling. "Here, let me move the stove."

He helped her find the ring and then went upstairs. He expected Melanie to be waiting for him. But when he stepped into his room, the window was open. Melanie had climbed out. She was gone.

Kaz turned toward his desk. He stopped cold when he saw the message scrawled on the mirror over his dresser. Melanie had written it in magic marker. Kaz began to tremble as he read the words she had scrawled.

DATE THIS, LOVER BOY.

Kaz grabbed a cloth to wipe the words off the mirror. He wondered if Melanie had seen him with Tiffany. He could still hear her voice on the phone machine.

*You better not be out with another girl. I'll kill you if you are.*

DATE THIS, LOVER BOY.

It was the second time he had wiped these words from a mirror.

Meanwhile, Marcia Granholm sat in front of the television waiting for the local news to come on.

Perhaps they would have further information regarding the murder of Carol Ledbetter. But she was disappointed. The report was just a rehash of the horrifying details that were already familiar to her. She remembered the fight in the hallway, when Carol had been screaming. That hadn't been mentioned in the report. There had been no mention of Kaz, either.

Marcia began to tremble. Everyone had seen Kaz arguing with Carol on Monday. And Kaz had been called to Mr. Lipton's office.

"No, he couldn't do it!"

The report said that there were no suspects in the case, not so far. If Kaz had been guilty of something like that, they would have arrested him. Still, Marcia had to wonder how serious his relationship had been with Carol.

"He couldn't!"

"Marcia, honey?"

She looked up to see her father. "Hi, Daddy."

"Are you okay? You look spooked."

Marcia sighed. "A girl was killed. One of my classmates."

Her father grimaced. He asked her all about the girl and she told him what she knew. But it wasn't much, considering that she left out all information about Kaz.

"You be careful, Marcia," he warned. "It seems to me this girl was probably running around with the wrong crowd."

When he left the room, Marcia switched off the television. She knew Kaz couldn't have killed

Carol. Kaz was a lot of things, but he was not a killer.

Marcia wanted to call him, but she hesitated. She had to have a plan. She knew that Kaz had been called into Mr. Lipton's office, and that he had been questioned by a police officer. If she were in his position, she would assume the worst—that she was a suspect. Now that Kaz was in such desperate straits, he would need all the help he could get. Marcia believed with all her heart that if she could help Kaz prove his innocence and, while doing so, find the killer, he would at last recognize her love for him.

She picked up the phone and dialed his private number. Kaz answered on the first ring.

"Hello," he said.

She could feel the panic in his voice. Who was he expecting to call him?

"Hello! Hello!" he called into the phone.

Holding her breath, Marcia hung up. She had found out what she needed to know. Kaz was at home. Now she could start to help him.

After another sleepless night, Kaz had to get through the school day. He staggered from class to class, wondering all the time what he could do to find Carol's killer. He suspected Melanie, at least until he saw Ricky Buller glaring at him in the hallway.

Maybe Ricky was the killer. Melanie's hateful message could have been a coincidence. Or maybe they were working together. After all, they both hated him.

Kaz could not wait for the day to end. But fifth period came and the announcement blared over the loudspeaker. The fifth-period class had been canceled so everyone could report to the gym for a memorial service in honor of Carol Ledbetter.

Kaz had to sit in the bleachers, listening to the speech by Henry Lipton. A pastor from a local church also spoke. The final words came from Sheriff Hagen, who pleaded for information that might put him on the path of the killer.

When the ceremony was over, Kaz had to sit through sixth period. He didn't hear a word of the teacher's presentation. His eyes kept flickering to the clock on the wall. He wanted to go home.

The bell finally rang, freeing him from the torture. He ran to his car. The Miata roared through the streets of Cresswell. Kaz drove back to Rocky Bank Estates and hurried into his house.

In his room, he felt safe for a moment. He fell back on the bed, looking up at the ceiling. He lay there for a long time before he drifted into a fitful slumber. Tossing and turning from his nightmares, he woke later to the darkness of the night.

A thumping noise had awakened him. Kaz opened his eyes. The breeze blew the curtains away from his window. He thought he heard someone dropping to the ground below his room.

"Who's there?"

He hurried to the casement, peering out into the shadows. Was that a dark shape sliding over the high wooden fence in his backyard? Kaz hurried downstairs. He asked his mother if anyone had come to see him. His mother said that no one had called.

Kaz went back to his room. He switched on the light. It was then that he saw the Cresswell High yearbook lying on the floor.

The yearbook did not belong to Kaz. Since he had arrived so late in the year, he had not purchased an annual. Someone had thrown the book through his open window.

Kaz lifted the book from the floor. His stomach was turning. He was afraid to open it. But he had to have a look.

With trembling hands, Kaz began to turn the pages. Maybe the yearbook was somebody's idea of a joke. But what did it mean?

He got to the pictures of the seniors. He flipped to the page with the picture of Carol Ledbetter. Kaz almost dropped the book. Carol's picture had been crossed out with a big, red $X$.

"No."

Quickly, he thumbed through the alphabetical listings until he got to Sally Thornton. He was hoping that her picture would be clear. But there was another red $X$ crossed through the smiling face.

"Sally!"

Kaz began to get a sick feeling in his stomach. An intense sensation of fear washed over him. The pain shot through his abdomen, gripping him like the shredding claws of a wild animal.

He picked up the phone, dialing Sally's number. But there was no answer. Kaz hung up. He had to get to her house. He had to make sure that Sally was not the next victim of the killer.

# Chapter 11

Kaz rushed out of the house and climbed into his Miata. He backed out of the driveway and raced away toward the entrance of Rocky Bank Estates. It was almost seven-thirty. He didn't notice the gray Toyota Camry following him at a cautious distance.

As he raced out of Rocky Bank Estates, tearing through Pelham Four Corners, Kaz was calculating Sally's schedule. She usually worked at the record shop until eight or nine, depending on whether or not she was supposed to close the store. So it made sense that she would not have answered the phone when Kaz called. Maybe she wasn't home yet. Kaz would have been elated to find an empty house.

Kaz shuddered when he realized that he had not looked at any of the other pictures in the yearbook. What if Tiffany's picture had been crossed out? No, he had looked through the K section, and he had not seen an *X* on those pages.

He rounded a sharp turn, squealing the tires on the road. He was on Broad Street leading into the Upper Basin. When he straightened out the Miata, flashing lights appeared behind him. The patrol car had come out of nowhere.

Kaz figured the deputy had been waiting for him. This was all part of their strategy of entrapment. Some clue that he had overlooked was going to nail him.

Kaz pulled over to the breakdown lane. He watched as a tall deputy got out of the patrol car. The law officer came toward the Miata with a walkie-talkie in hand. The radio crackled threateningly, and Kaz sighed in frustration. This would delay his arrival at Sally's.

The gray Toyota passed by slowly. Marcia saw Kaz presenting his license and registration to the officer. She drove on slowly, observing the scene as best she could in her rearview mirror. If he was on Broad Street in the Upper Basin, there was only one place he could be going. Marcia flipped open the notebook that was on the seat beside her. Using her access to the school registrar's files, she had written down the addresses of all of Kaz's girlfriends. Next to Sally's name she had written, "Lives w/ aunt—230 Haskell Ave., off Broad." Haskell Avenue was coming up. She would be at Sally's in just a couple of minutes.

"You were going mighty fast, kid," the deputy said.

Kaz nodded. "Yes, sir. I'm sorry."

"So you admit you were speeding?" the officer asked.

"Yes, sir. Isn't that why you stopped me?"

"Let me have a look at your license, kid. Routine check."

Kaz fumbled for his wallet. He gave his driver's license to the officer. This was it. Once the positive identification was made, he would find a reason to take Kaz into custody. Then they would find a way to blame him for killing Carol.

The deputy shook his head and grunted. He moved around behind the car with the walkie-talkie chattering in his hand. He turned a flashlight beam on the Miata's license plate.

Kaz felt a cramp in his side. He could hear the cell door clanking shut on him. He would have to reveal everything when he was arrested, including the crossed-out faces in the yearbook. At least they could send a patrol car to check on Sally.

The deputy came toward him. "Here's the deal, Mr. Kasden. I'm going to give you a break on the speeding. You're a polite young man, and you admitted your mistake."

Kaz hesitated. Maybe he wasn't going to be arrested. Unless the law officer was simply toying with him.

"Thank you, sir. May I go?"

"Not yet. Wayne, are you living in Cresswell on a permanent basis?"

"Yes, sir. In Rocky Bank Estates."

"So you moved here from Florida. I mean, you have a Florida tag and a Florida driver's license."

"Yes, sir."

"How long have you been in Cresswell?"

Kaz shrugged, wiping the sweat from his forehead. "Less than a month."

The deputy nodded and gave him back his license. "Well, I'm not going to give you a ticket for speeding. But as a new resident, you have four weeks to register your car and get a new license. Next time I see you, you'd better be square."

Kaz smiled nervously. "Thank you, sir. I'll take care of it. You know how it is. I haven't had the time to get a new license."

"Better make time."

"Yes, sir."

The deputy went back to the patrol car. Ten or fifteen minutes had been lost. Kaz drove two blocks down and stopped at the nearest telephone.

Sally Thornton trudged wearily up the steps of her Upper Basin home. The house was completely dark. Sally turned the key in the lock, wondering why her aunt had not left the porch light on. She stepped into the deep shadows.

"Aunt Sarah?"

But there was no reply from the empty rooms. Sally turned on a hall light. She moved toward the kitchen, flipping another light switch as soon as she got there. She saw the note on the refrigerator. Her aunt had gone out earlier that evening, while Sally was still at work. According to the note, her aunt would return soon. She had gone to the movies with some friends.

"Glad someone is having a good time," Sally muttered to herself.

Pulling open the refrigerator door, Sally grabbed a soda and sat down at the kitchen table. She was tired and depressed. And the reason for her despondency was clear as the name formed on her lips.

"Kaz, you jerk."

She relived the scene in the hall, when she had berated him for going out with another girl. The whole thing had left a bad feeling inside her. The gnawing in her heart wouldn't go away.

She knew that Kaz had been two-timing her. He had been seen at the beach with some blonde. It was all over school, along with the rumor that Kaz had been seeing Carol Ledbetter, the girl who had been killed.

No one had been arrested yet for her murder. But Sally was not prepared to have a reputation for having dated a murderer. She was not about to say that Kaz wasn't capable of such a heinous deed. He was a two-timer, he was deceitful, he was manipulative, he was a phony. Why couldn't he be a killer as well?

She had told him off, let him know what she thought of him. Now she could forget him and hope that her name would never ever be connected with his.

But chill bumps crept over her skin when she remembered his touch, his kiss. No boy had ever excited her like Kaz. It would be difficult to let him go.

Rising from the table, Sally dragged herself toward the stairs. As she started up the steps, she thought she heard a creaking noise above her. Sally stopped in the shadows. The upper floor was still dark.

"Aunt Sarah?"

Maybe her aunt had come home early. But there was no reply. And the old house was quiet again.

"This dump is always making noise."

Sally continued upward, climbing into blackness. She wanted to take a shower and go to bed. She was looking forward to a good night's sleep.

The scent of potpourri greeted her as she slipped into her room. Sally undressed and put on a thin robe. She sat for a moment at her vanity, taking off her makeup. Her face looked tired and pale.

"Kaz. Kaz the . . . spaz. Who am I kidding? Kaz the hunk."

She sighed and opened a drawer in the vanity. She took out a diary that had been bound in a lavender cover. Grabbing a pen, Sally began to write her entry for the day.

Work stunk. I'm always thinking about Kaz. It felt good when I told him off, but now it feels horrible. Like it or not, I'm still hung up on Kaz. It upsets me to think I won't be seeing him. We never talked about going steady, so I guess I didn't have the right to expect him to go out with just me. We didn't have any kind of understanding. And I did spend time with a couple of other guys. Of course, they didn't thrill me like Kaz. Now he's a suspect in the Carol Ledbetter case—at least he's been questioned, and he was seeing her, too, so in my mind he's a suspect. I've got to watch out for myself and stay away from him—until this blows over. . . .

Sally put the diary on her vanity, leaving it open. Rising from the vanity, she was startled by the ringing of her telephone. Maybe it was her aunt.

She picked up the phone after the first ring.

"Hello," she said.

"Sally, you can't stay there another minute," commanded a frantic voice at the other end of the line. "Leave your house. Leave right now, this minute. Someone is after you. I was trying to warn you in person, but the police stopped me for speeding."

"What are you talking about, Kaz? Calm down." She had never heard him sound so crazy before. It scared her.

"I can't calm down!" Kaz bellowed from the other end of the wire. "Somebody is going to try to kill you! It's the same person who killed Carol!"

Sally was skeptical. Was this some kind of a setup? "How do you know all this?" she demanded.

"I'll explain it all to you," he shouted. "Just get out now. Listen, it's ten till eight. Meet me at eight at the northwest corner of Grant's Park."

Sally grabbed a tube of lipstick and began to write on a piece of her stationery. That was when she felt the rope of cloth around her neck. She began to gag and fight for her life as the phone dropped from her hand.

Sally never felt the sharp steel that ripped across her throat, and she never saw the fingers that dipped into the crimson puddle and scrawled the hateful message on the wall above her body.

# Chapter 12

Marcia parked her car a short distance from Sally's house on Haskell Avenue. The houses were mostly two and three story, separated from one another by a hedge on one side and a driveway on the other. There were lights on in most of the windows, but there was no sound emanating from any of the houses except for the occasional slam of a screen door or the thud of something being thrown into a garbage can or the pleading sound of a telephone ringing.

Marcia watched number 230 intently. It was a white, two-story house. There was a light on downstairs, shining dimly from one of the back rooms. Upstairs, there were lights on in one of the bedrooms. Marcia could detect a figure going back and forth in front of the window.

She kept watching the street for any sign of Kaz. She jumped when headlights beamed on her and seemed to linger a moment too long. But it was just a car passing on the cross street. Marcia wasn't sure what she would do if she saw Kaz now. She wasn't really sure why she had parked outside Sally Thornton's house. All she knew was that Kaz was in trouble, and she wanted to help him and have him all to herself. Soon enough he would realize that she was the only one who really loved him.

Suddenly, something caught her eye. The light was flickering in the bedroom window. It got brighter for just a split second and then dimmer. A shadow darted past the window.

Marcia eased herself from her car. She scurried up to the hedge, which bordered the small front yard, and listened intently. She looked all around to make sure nobody had seen her. If someone appeared, she was prepared to walk along the sidewalk as if nothing unusual were happening.

Then, from within the house, Marcia could hear racing footsteps. The back door was opened and shut quickly and carefully. Marcia stooped down and raced around behind the hedge. There were quick footsteps on the cement walk behind Sally's house. Marcia could hear a rear gate being guided open. Then she heard someone running as fast as they could. Her heart was racing. This was her opportunity. She ran through the neighbor's backyard and opened the rear gate. It opened onto a wide, unlighted alley. Whoever had just raced down it was nowhere to be seen.

Marcia waited, not sure what to do. She knew in her heart that something terrible had just happened, but she was too terrified to find out what it was. Where was Kaz? How long had it been since she had passed him on Broad Street, where he had been pulled over by the policeman. Five minutes? Ten minutes? It was hard to tell. Had he been taken in by the police? At least there would be ironclad proof of his whereabouts during the incident at Sally's.

Marcia scurried back to her car and drove home. It was time to call the police and give them an anonymous tip.

# Chapter 13

The Miata skidded to a halt in front of Sally's house. Kaz jumped out and ran up the walk. He prayed that he wasn't too late. The house was dim inside. A light burned in the front hall and somewhere in one of the rear rooms. There was a light on in the bedroom upstairs.

Kaz banged on the front door. "Sally? Sally, are you in there?"

There was no answer. He could still hear himself screaming into the dead phone.

Kaz felt his heart thumping as he tried the doorknob. It was open. He pushed into the narrow hallway.

"Sally?"

When he emerged from the front hallway, he looked all around, but saw nothing unusual. Then he bounded up the stairs. He ran into Sally's room and stopped suddenly.

"No!"

Kaz bent down to feel for a pulse. His fingers touched the gaping crevice in her neck. He jumped back.

His head was spinning. What was he going to

do? He glanced up at the wall. The color drained from his face.

Someone had left a message over Sally's body. It resembled the words he had found on the mirror in Carol's room. The message had been scrawled in Sally's blood.

ALL YOURS, LOVER BOY.

The phone was off the hook. Next to the phone was a piece of stationery. Sally had written "8:00 at the" and nothing more. She had written it in lipstick. It was just like Sally. Kaz's eyes filled with tears, and fear suddenly gripped his chest.

Crazy with grief and rage, Kaz staggered down the stairs and out to the back alley. Maybe he would find something there that would lead him to the murderer.

Kaz pulled himself to the top of a fence. He peered toward a well-lit street corner. But it was foolish. There was nothing to be gained by racing about aimlessly. He had to get control of himself. He knew he was starting to panic, and that could lead him into making a big mistake.

He had to get back to the house. There was a dead girl lying on the floor of her bedroom. He had to figure out what to do.

As he limped back through the alley, a beam of light shined down on him. Kaz gazed up into the blinding glare. His face was illuminated in the glow.

"Who's there?" someone called from a second-story window that overlooked the alley. "What are you doing?"

He turned his face away from the light, moving

toward the back steps of Sally's house. The light followed him for a moment and then disappeared. Kaz climbed the steps and moved through the kitchen. He returned to the nightmare that awaited him.

Sally lay motionless in the blood. Her body was a twisted heap. The red liquid had thickened, congealing into a slick mirror.

Kaz lifted his eyes to the message on the wall. What was he going to do? He wasn't thinking straight. His head whirled like a carnival ride. Sweat poured off his face. He was going to throw up.

One of the neighbors had seen him in the alley. His face had been clear in the beam of light. But he had only looked up for a moment. Maybe the person wouldn't be able to identify him.

He had to clear out quickly. But first he had to wash the bloody message from the wall.

Kaz hurried downstairs to the kitchen, looking for some soap and a bucket. He found a sponge and dishwashing liquid. There was a big pot on the stove. Kaz filled it with water and squirted in the soap.

He carried the pot of water up the stairs. When he dipped the sponge into the soapy liquid, he felt stupid. He should just leave. That would be the best thing to do.

"I've got to get out of here," he mumbled to himself.

But when he turned toward the bedroom door, there was someone there. It was too late. He could never make things right.

The woman's shrieking rose in the night. Sally's aunt wore the most horrible expression he had ever seen in his life. She was staring straight at Kaz.

"Murderer! You killed her! Sally!"

Kaz made a bad choice. He pushed her aside and ran past her. He bolted down the stairs and burst through the back door, all to the sound of her anguished screams.

He ran quickly through the alley. When he knocked over the garbage can, the flashlight came back, swirling over the alley like a prison search beam.

"Who's there? What are you doing?"

Kaz turned the corner, running out of the beam. He could still hear the screaming of Sally's aunt. Her desperate cries pierced the night.

"Murderer! He killed her! She's dead. My Sally is dead."

Kaz had to get away. They would never believe him. They would never believe that someone was framing him. He had to stay free and find a way to clear himself.

He ran as fast as he could down the alley. His plan was to double back down the street to his car and drive away. But Kaz froze as the shrill cry of sirens rose suddenly in the night. He saw the flashing reflections of patrol cars in the distance. They were already on their way to Sally's.

"I'm dead."

Two people had seen him. One of the neighbors had flashed a light directly upon his face. Sally's aunt had witnessed him standing over the body. He was sunk in the water.

But he couldn't give up, not yet. He had to hide. If he could stay on his own for a while, he might find a way to turn the tables on whoever was trying to frame him.

He knew he couldn't stay in the neighborhood. The place was going to be crawling with police. He had to keep moving. He turned south, making for the Lower Basin.

Kaz had never been in the seedier sections of Cresswell. He found the narrow streets forbidding. He descended into an area of burned-out buildings and empty warehouses. There were few cars parked on the street, and those Kaz saw looked abandoned. He kept looking until he found a place that had a basement.

Slipping into the dark, smelly cellar, Kaz closed the rotten door behind him. As he made his way through piles of debris in the underground cell, he thought he heard rats chattering in the shadows. Something scurried along the floor, racing over his feet.

But Kaz did not care. He only wanted to sit for a moment by himself, to think of what he should do. He found an old paint can, turned it over, and sat down. His feet sloshed in an oily puddle. Tears fell from his eyes. He whispered Sally's name.

Outside, the faint whine of sirens filtered through the lonely darkness of Cresswell.

# Chapter 14

Marcia Granholm's eyes were riveted to the flashing screen of the color television. She was watching the morning news. The anchorwoman's clear voice came out of the small speaker, relaying the horrible account of Sally Thornton's murder.

". . . body was found late last night by the girl's aunt, Mrs. Sarah Hunter, who had returned home just moments before the killer fled. Apparently Mrs. Hunter surprised the killer, who was standing over the body. Sally Thornton had been strangled, and her throat had been cut. She was in her bedroom. . . ."

The visual image switched to an exterior view of the neat, white house. The front yard had been roped off by the sheriff. Marcia grimaced, but she kept her eyes on the screen.

"This bloody spectacle is the second murder of this type to occur in Cresswell within the span of one week. However, unlike the first murder, this time the killer left behind a message. We now switch to Kristy Whitaker on the scene of the bizarre killing. Kristy."

A red-haired woman was standing in front of a remote camera. Behind her were the words that had been written in blood. Marcia could not tear herself away.

"As you can see, after Sally Thornton was slain, the murderer left behind this inscription, which appears to be written in the dead girl's own blood. The words *All yours, lover boy,* along with an eyewitness identification, have led Sheriff Tommy Hagen to search for a young man by the name of Wayne Kasden, who just moved to Rocky Bank Estates from Jacksonville, Florida. The girl's diary and a piece of paper that she is believed to have been writing on at the time of her murder have been removed by the sheriff's department for examination. Exactly what Sally Thornton was writing remains a mystery at this hour."

Marcia was terrified. She had been only fifty feet from the scene of the crime. She had heard the murderer's footsteps. She had called the police.

"Mr. Kasden, known sometimes as Kaz, was reportedly discovered standing over the body of Sally Thornton just as her aunt came home from an evening at the movies with friends. . . ."

"It can't be," Marcia said. "He didn't do it." But as she said this, Marcia began to have doubts. Maybe he had seen her parked outside Sally's house. Maybe he had snuck around to the back to do his evil deed. But how does one explain the fact that he was discovered by Sally's aunt? Had he snuck back into the house to retrieve a piece of evidence he had forgotten?

A photo of Kaz flashed on the screen.

"Wayne 'Kaz' Kasden was supposedly seeing

Carol Ledbetter, along with several other girls at Cresswell . . ."

"Not me. Keep me out of it," Marcia pleaded quietly to the television.

"Kasden's red Miata was found in front of the house by deputies who arrived on the scene just moments before he fled."

Marcia did not want to believe that Kaz would kill anyone.

Marcia shook her head. *Maybe he was there to warn Sally,* she thought. *Would anyone believe me if I came forward and said I was following Kaz, and that I had heard someone running from the house at least five minutes before Kaz was discovered? No one would believe me. I'd look like a fool, and I'd never have a boyfriend for the rest of my life.*

"One eyewitness saw Kasden leaving the scene through the alley behind Miss Thornton's Upper Basin home. . . ."

The visual image switched to Miss Ida Mae Freeman, an older woman with curlers in her gray hair.

". . . right there in the alley. I shined my light on him and asked him what he was doing there. I remember what he looked like because he was such a handsome boy."

Marcia just stared blankly at the television.

The anchorwoman came back on the screen. "Kristy, the Sheriff's Department has certainly released a lot more details in this case, many more than they did in the case of Carol Ledbetter."

Marcia flinched. She saw Carol arguing with

Kaz. She remembered the story about Sally telling him off. But would that drive Kaz to kill them?

"Sheriff Hagen is certain that Kasden is the one who killed both girls. The town of Cresswell has offered a five-thousand-dollar reward for anyone who comes forward in this case and leads them to Kasden's arrest. . . ."

*He's still free,* Marcia thought. *He's out there somewhere, alone and frightened.* But what could she do to help him?

"Classes have been canceled for the rest of the week due to the horrors that have plagued this otherwise normal high school. . . ."

Marcia switched off the television. She was stunned. She shuddered at the thought of the message that had been written in blood.

*All yours, lover boy.*

Why would Kaz write something so bizarre?

"Marcia, honey?"

Her father was standing at the doorway.

"Hi, Dad."

"School was canceled," he told her.

"I know, Dad."

He frowned at her. "Honey, they're saying this boy, Kasden, killed two girls. Wasn't he the one you were dating?"

"I went out with him once," Marcia replied. "But we—I mean, he wasn't really my type."

"Thank heaven for that. Honey, I know this isn't an easy time for you. If you want, I'll call the office and tell them I won't be in—"

Marcia shook her head. "No, I'll be all right."

"What about this boy? They haven't found him yet."

"He won't bother me," Marcia replied. "He doesn't even know I'm alive. Besides, I don't think he did it anyway."

When her father had gone, Marcia looked out the window. It was a gray morning with the threat of rain. Clouds were sweeping over Cresswell. Kaz was out there somewhere. Marcia knew he was innocent. She could feel it.

There had to be something she could do to help him.

# Chapter 15

Kaz opened his eyes when he heard the baying dog. He had been in the basement all night and most of the morning. It wasn't dark outside, but it was a gray day as the rain had been coming down since about three in the morning.

"Look over there," a loud voice called. "I think there's a basement in that one."

Kaz felt a tightness all over his body. They were using a hound to look for him, to find his trail. He would be discovered.

He began to look around the basement. He found a big pipe that receded into the wall. It was wide enough for him to crawl into it. But the hound would still be able to smell him.

Kaz felt something oozing beneath his feet. It was too dark to tell whether it was mud or sludge or some form of toxic waste. Whatever it was, the stench from the stuff was horrible.

"Hey, here's a doorway," the deputy called. "I'm going down."

Kaz quickly scooped up two handfuls of the ooze. He crawled back into the pipe and then smeared the mud all over the opening. The basement door opened slowly. Kaz lowered his face, covering his head with his hands as the deputy led the dog into the cellar.

Kaz could hear the hound whining. It stopped in front of the pipe, sniffing and yelping. The deputy swung his flashlight. The beam washed over the pipe.

"Stinks, huh. What is it, boy?"

Kaz heard a rat squeaking in the pipe. Suddenly the rodent ran over him. They were two rats in a hole. Kaz swiped at the animal, knocking it out of the pipe. The hound went crazy when the rat hit the floor.

"Whatcha got, Charlie?" came a gruff voice from across the basement.

"Ah, just a rat. Come on, Gomer," he said to the dog. "Let's beat it. There's nothing down here but mud and rats."

Kaz listened to them as they left. He waited for a long time before he crawled out of the pipe. When he did, he resumed his position on the paint can. His stomach felt hollow. He was desperately thirsty, but he was too nervous to eat. The minutes crept by. He was waiting for the evening shadows to grow long over Cresswell. Then he could move about in the safety of night.

Kaz had already decided that there was only one place for him to go. He would have to be careful along the way. He just hoped she would take him in once he got there.

All morning and afternoon, as he sat in the dark, fetid basement, he recounted every moment he had spent with each of the girls who had dated him. The murderer was one of the remaining girls.

Or it could be Ricky Buller. He had resented Kaz from the first day and had vowed revenge after Kaz had beaten him up. Then there was Melanie. She was as wild as a tomcat. She shoplifted with impunity and had even made veiled threats against Kaz if he two-timed her. And there was Tiffany. She was passionate and clinging in an obsessive way. There was a smouldering fire in her heart, but was she capable of murder? Kaz wasn't crossing her off the list. Then there was Marcia. She was so open and decent. Why hadn't he given her a chance? He hoped that now she would give him one.

# Chapter 16

The rain fell harder on the streets of Cresswell. Marcia Granholm sat in her private study over the garage, listening to the drone of the downpour on the roof. It was dusk. Her father had just left for a bridge party. She was alone.

Marcia sighed and put aside the book she had been trying to read. Her thoughts had been dominated by the boy that she loved and the horror that had descended on Cresswell. Kaz couldn't have killed those girls. Marcia was sure of it.

True, he had gotten violent with Ricky Buller, dislocating his shoulder. But Ricky had been the one who started the fight. Ricky was more the type to hurt someone without provocation. Marcia had fended off Ricky's churlish advances. She had been lucky to get away from him unharmed.

Yet despite her faith in Kaz, Marcia could not escape from the fact that he had been seeing the other girls. He had been caught at Sally Thornton's house, standing over her body. He had also run away from the scene of the crime instead of remaining there to explain himself. But Marcia still could not picture him hurting anyone, especially one of the girls he had been dating.

Marcia stood up suddenly. If someone had been hurting Kaz's girlfriends, what would stop that person from coming after *her.* Suddenly she felt nervous. The killer could be stalking her right now!

Marcia went downstairs to make sure all the doors were locked.

She started for the door that opened onto a set of stairs that led down to the garage. From there she went out to the yard in order to push shut one of the breezeway jalousies. It was a constant nuisance. She would have to walk through the rain.

Marcia pushed open the door. The rain pelted her face. Marcia took one step out into the storm. She was reaching back to close the door when the hand closed over her mouth. Someone grabbed her from behind.

The hand muffled her screams. The intruder pushed her back inside. She heard the door slam shut. Marcia tried to struggle, but the intruder was too strong. She was going to die like the others.

"Don't worry," a familiar voice whispered in her ear. "I'm not going to hurt you. I'll let you go if you promise not to scream."

Marcia nodded. The hand fell away from her mouth. Marcia turned quickly to look at the pitiful figure in front of her. She almost didn't recognize him.

"Kaz, you look horrible!"

His face was dirty, his hands and clothes were covered with grime. His eyes were sunken and his hair was disheveled and oily. A foul stench issued from his body.

"Kaz—"

His steel blue eyes looked right through her. "Marcia, I came here because you're the only one I can turn to. I needed a place to go. Did you hear about me?"

She nodded. "Yes, I did."

"I didn't do it," he said desperately. "I swear."

She put her hand on his shoulder. "I believe you, Kaz. But you have to turn yourself in."

"I can't, Marcia. They'll never believe me. Someone set me up. And I think I know who did it."

"Who?"

"I'm not entirely sure, but I think it was Melanie Kaylor."

"Really?"

"Yes," Kaz replied. "I was seeing her, too."

He explained about Melanie's bent for larceny. He told her about Melanie's attack on him, the arrival of the yearbook with the crossed-out pictures, the way Melanie had used words similar to those left behind at the killings. Marcia listened patiently, her eyes growing narrow. She thought Kaz made sense.

"Kaz, you've got to go to the sheriff."

"He'll never believe me, Marcia. Sally's aunt saw me standing there. But I just went there to warn Sally. I got there too late. I came to warn you, too, Marcia. I need your help. You're the only one I can turn to."

"Kaz, I have a confession to make," Marcia said quietly. "I waited outside your house last night and then I followed you. I was the one who called and then hung up. I knew you didn't kill Carol Ledbetter. I wanted to help you." She felt as if she was pleading for him to understand her love for him. This was the moment she had rehearsed so many times in her heart.

She continued. "When you were stopped by the policeman on Broad Street, I continued on to Sally's. I knew where you were going. I had Sally's address. When I got to her house, I waited for a few minutes. There seemed to be a disturbance upstairs, so I ran through the neighbor's yard to the back. Somebody had run away. I couldn't see them. I know it wasn't you. You didn't show up until later. Isn't that right, Kaz?"

Kaz looked at her, amazed. "That's right. When I got there, it was too late. Oh, Marcia, can I really trust you?"

"Yes, Kaz, you're with me now. I'll help you," she said. She looked at his grime-encrusted face, but saw nothing but a look of shock there. "I'll help you, Kaz. All this time, I've wanted to be with you. I want to be your one true friend."

"I want to tell you everything, Marcia," he said. "I have to tell someone. It's about Tiffany—"

"Melanie's twin sister?"

Kaz nodded. "I've been seeing her, too. I'm worried, Marcia. Maybe she's involved. I can't rule her out."

Marcia had to ask one question. "Kaz, are you in love with Tiffany?"

"I don't know, Marcia. I just don't want anyone else to be hurt. Will you help me?"

"Kaz—"

"Please, Marcia. I want to make things right. I have to."

She couldn't resist his pleading tone. He was innocent. And Marcia could help him prove it. It was also her one chance to get close to him. But why didn't he embrace her after she had bared her soul to him? Why wasn't he as in love with her as she was in love with him? Did he suddenly think that she was the killer because she had been near Sally's house last night?

"Please help me, Marcia," he said.

"Of course I will, Kaz. But you've got to promise me one thing."

"Anything!"

"If we haven't found any evidence against Melanie or someone else by tomorrow, you have to turn yourself in."

He nodded. "I will. I promise."

"Come on. We have to get you cleaned up. There's a shower upstairs. I'll get some of my father's old clothes out of his closet."

"Thanks, Marcia."

When he had showered and changed clothes, they sat together on the couch. Kaz put his head in her lap. He closed his eyes as Marcia stroked his hair.

"I love you, Kaz."

But he had already fallen asleep.

Marcia sat there for a long time until the phone rang. It was her father. He wanted to make sure she was okay. As she looked at the frightened sleeping boy on the couch, she assured her father that she was.

When she had hung up, she looked at Kaz again. He seemed so peaceful. She kissed his forehead and told him that she loved him once again.

# Chapter 17

Kaz cried out and sat up on the sofa. There were shadows all around him. He was disoriented, not sure where he had been resting. He saw a dark shape moving toward him.

"Stay away from me!" he cried.

"Kaz, it's me. Marcia!"

The whole thing came rushing back to him in one long stream of memory. He saw her long brown hair and her kind face. He wiped the sweat from his forehead.

"Sorry, I—"

Marcia knelt down next to him. "Kaz, it's all right."

He threw his arms around her. "Marcia, thank God you're alive. I dreamed that you had been killed, too."

Marcia closed her eyes as they embraced. He felt so warm. She desperately wanted him to love her. But there were still too many obstacles in the way. Marcia hoped she could fix that.

She drew back, trying to smile at him. "Kaz, I have to go out."

He looked into her eyes, showing his fears. "Why?"

"I'm going to spy on Melanie," she replied. "If you think she's responsible for killing those girls—"

"No, you can't do it!"

"Kaz, I don't have any choice. It's the only way. If you go out, you'll be spotted."

"Melanie is dangerous," Kaz replied. "You can't go by yourself, Marcia. You just can't."

"I'm just going to watch her. I won't do anything else. I promise. She won't even know I'm there."

Kaz took her hand. "I screwed up, Marcia. I screwed up bad. I can't let you fix my mistakes."

"Kaz, I—I love you. And I want you to love me."

"I do—"

"Don't say it unless you mean it, Kaz."

He kissed her lightly on the lips. "I mean it, Marcia. You're the only one who matters to me now."

"What about Tiffany?"

Kaz sighed. "I just want to save her life."

"Right now it's more important that we save you," she said. "The police are looking all over for you. Somebody is trying to frame you. I have to find that person. If you go out with me now, they'll arrest you. Wait in the study. My father rarely goes in there. Just don't make noise. I'll be back soon. I promise."

He smiled. "All right, Marcia. Just be careful."

She patted his hand. "I will."

"Marcia, where are you going to begin?"

"I'm going to drive over to Melanie's house," she replied.

"Do you know where Melanie lives?"

"I got her address from the registrar's office. She lives in the Upper Basin. It's not that far. My neighborhood is technically Gaspee Farms, but it's really closer to the Basin. We're right on the border."

Kaz gazed adoringly at her.

Marcia wondered if the look was sincere. She started to turn away.

"Marcia?"

She looked back at his handsome, expectant face. "Yes?"

"You wouldn't turn me in, would you?"

"If I was going to do that," she replied, "I would have called the sheriff while you were sleeping. I'll be back soon. Remember, if my father comes home, stay absolutely quiet. I left him a note saying I went to a friend's house. There's a phone extension in the study. Don't answer unless I make my signal. I'll ring once, hang up, and then ring again."

He watched her go out the door. She was being too good to him. He didn't deserve her, even if she was his only hope.

Marcia guided the gray Toyota to a halt across the street from Melanie's house. The rain had finally stopped. Evening shadows were long over the Upper Basin. A few dim lights burned on the second floor. Marcia turned off the engine and began to watch the house. She didn't have to wait long before something strange happened.

A black pickup truck rolled to a stop directly in front of the house. Marcia gaped as Ricky Buller got out. He walked to the front door and knocked.

Melanie answered the door with a bright smile and let him inside.

Marcia's heart was pumping. It was obvious now that two people with such evil dispositions would find each other. Ricky Buller and Melanie Kaylor! Who would have believed it? Marcia couldn't have imagined two more formidable adversaries.

After ten minutes of anguished waiting, the door opened once again. Ricky and Melanie stepped out of the house together. They looked around suspiciously, not seeing Marcia just twenty feet away, and got into the black truck. It roared to life and pulled away from the curb. Marcia was so nervous that she could barely get the key in the ignition. But she finally put the car into gear and started to follow them.

# Chapter 18

Kaz was boiling inside. He felt helpless. Almost an hour had passed. All he could do was sit and wait for Marcia to come back or call. He didn't know who he loved right now. He just wanted an end to this misery. His parents were probably going crazy with fright. But he couldn't go home until his name was cleared.

He thought he had been a fool to drop a girl like Marcia. He never should have let her fall by the wayside. She was a good person. Marcia wouldn't have gotten him into so much trouble. She had been his first girlfriend in Cresswell. He should have stuck to her and only her.

Kaz began to pace around the room. Marcia was a smart girl. She wouldn't let Melanie see her. But what could she find out? Melanie was probably lying low for a while. Then an evil thought invaded his mind. Maybe Marcia was the killer. He had seen how obsessive her love for him was. Would she kill in order to have him all to herself? No! No! He couldn't bear to think about that possibility.

He looked at the clock on the wall. It was after seven. He switched on a radio next to the chair where he had been sitting. But he couldn't listen when the newscaster reported him still at large and possibly dangerous.

By eight o'clock, he was ready to go looking for Marcia.

Marcia followed the truck for a half hour. It was heading south, out of town. Ricky and Melanie pulled over twice at convenience stores. They would both go in and appear a few minutes later carrying a small bag. Marcia was sure that Melanie was stealing things while Ricky distracted the person at the register. What a dope! She could see how he would be attracted to someone like Melanie.

At Creighton Woods, a large park south of town, the truck turned down a back road. Marcia hung back, pulling the Toyota off to the side of the road. She could see the truck's headlights deep within the forest. The truck had stopped. What were they doing? Did they figure out she was following them? Marcia waited.

After a few minutes, she backed up to a phone booth she had spotted about a hundred yards back. She got out of her car. The world around her was absolutely silent. The car's engine, now turned off, emitted a reassuring ticking noise. She dialed her number, let it ring once, then hung up. She prayed that her father wasn't home yet. She needed Kaz. When she dialed again, he picked up on the first ring.

"Marcia?"

"Kaz, you'll never believe it. Ricky Buller picked up Melanie at her house. I've been following them."

"Where are you?"

"Near a place called Creighton Woods," Marcia replied. "Ricky drove his truck into the trees. I can't figure out what they're doing?"

"Where are you calling from?"

"There's a pay phone on the main road. There's an ice cream place here, but it doesn't open until after Memorial Day. The phone still works."

"Where are Ricky and Melanie?" he asked nervously.

"In the woods, like I told you. There's a dirt road here. It leads almost all the way to the cliffs."

"Cliffs?"

"On the east shore of Lighthouse Bay," she replied.

"Near Indian Point?"

"No, in the other direction. Lighthouse Bay is big. It curves around a long way."

"Okay," Kaz said. "Give me directions."

"Kaz, you can't. It's a long way."

"I'll figure out a way to get there." He was speaking quickly, frantically. "Marcia, don't go near them. Just stay where you are and tell me how to get there."

Marcia sighed. "Okay. You know the road that goes out to Indian Point?"

"Yes, state road 104, something like that."

"204," she corrected. "But instead of going on to Indian Point, you take 204A. That will bring you around the long way, to Creighton Woods. It's about ten miles outside of town. The turnoff is marked clearly."

"Listen Marcia, I'm worried. Why don't you get out of there. Come back and pick me up."

Marcia didn't have a chance to answer. She heard a rustling behind her, and then a rope was thrown over her head, and she was yanked by her neck away from the phone.

"Marcia!" Kaz cried from the other end of the line. "Marcia! Marcia, are you there?"

Marcia fought with all her might. She reached for her attacker's head and grabbed a handful of long hair. She pulled the head around in front of her. At that moment, before the knife was thrust into her throat, she saw the flawless complexion and perfect features that were the envy of every girl at Cresswell High.

"Tiffany," she gasped. Tiffany had brighter, more direct eyes than her sister. Marcia knew this, even at the moment of her death.

"Yes, it's me," hissed the beautiful girl. "Don't think I haven't followed your every footstep. None of you ever fooled me for a minute."

She dragged the lifeless body into the tall grass at the side of the road and disappeared into the night.

# Chapter 19

Kaz pumped the pedals of the bicycle, moving as fast as his aching legs would let him. He had found Marcia's bike in the garage below the private study. It had taken him almost an hour to find his way to Creighton Woods. A full moon had risen to light the road. He could finally see the ice cream stand ahead of him. The Toyota was parked by the phone booth.

He could barely get his breath as he climbed off the bicycle. He managed to call Marcia's name. There was only silence under the glow of the moon. Kaz began to step toward the ice cream stand. He noticed signs of a scuffle in the dirt.

"Marcia! No!"

Kaz moved slowly, scanning the ground. He went around the side of the ice cream stand. He started poking around in the tall grass. His feet tripped on something, and he tumbled to the ground. As he scrambled to regain his balance, he saw the pale face gaping at him.

"Marcia! Oh, no. No!"

Her eyes were open. But she was not looking at him. He touched her neck to feel for a pulse. His fingertips penetrated the opening in her throat. It had been sliced from ear to ear.

"Marcia, I'm sorry. I—"

He choked on the words. Tears spilled out of his eyes. She had died because of him. He had killed her.

Kaz stood up. His legs were weak. His whole body trembled. Marcia still gaped at him. She had died with her eyes open. She had died with her heart full of love for him.

It was time for Kaz to end it. He had to call the sheriff. He had to make things right, even if no one believed him.

Staggering past the Toyota, he reached for the pay phone. His hand shook as he put the phone to his ear. There was a dial tone, so he did not need a coin to dial the emergency number. He was lifting his other hand when the screaming resounded from the woods. He had forgotten all about the black truck that Marcia had been following.

A girl's shrieking rose in the moonlit night. The clamor was coming from the woods. The girl was crying for someone to help her.

Kaz's eyes grew wide. "Buller!"

They were still in there. Ricky was going to kill Melanie. That had to be who was screaming. Ricky was going to finish her so she couldn't finger him as an accomplice. Or maybe he had just flipped out completely.

The cry came through the trees again. Kaz peered toward the forest. He could not let another girl die, even if it was Melanie. He had to help.

Kaz ran to the Toyota. The keys were still in the

ignition. Kaz started the car and pulled onto the road. He drove slowly as he looked for an entrance into the woods. He finally saw the dirt road leading back through the trees. He drove into Creighton Woods.

The headlights flickered as the car bumped on the dirt road. Kaz had not gone far when he saw the black pickup truck in front of him. He got out, leaving on the car's headlights.

As he started for the truck, he saw a shape coming straight at him from behind a tree. Kaz jumped back. Ricky Buller staggered in his direction.

"Back off, Ricky! I mean it!"

But Ricky did not stop. He kept coming. Kaz struck a fighting stance. But he never had to throw a punch. Ricky fell forward, smashing face first into the dirt. A long knife blade protruded from his back.

Kaz gaped at the blood that poured from the wound. The no-necked bully twitched as the life left his body. Kaz heard the rasping of the death rattle.

"Help me!" Ricky moaned. "She's going to kill us all."

"Who is, Ricky?" Kaz asked, kneeling down.

"Tif—," was all he managed to say before his body went limp.

Kaz lifted his eyes. Shapes squirmed in the headlights. Blond hair flashed under the bright beams. He saw their faces. They were identical. The twins were fighting.

Had Ricky tried to say Tiffany? No, that couldn't be true. Somehow Melanie and Ricky had kidnapped Tiffany and brought her to the woods. Now Melanie was trying to kill her. Kaz saw a flash of polished metal in the beam of the headlights. The killer had also brought a gun.

"Help me, Kaz!"

Kaz tried to get closer. He had to take the weapon away from Melanie. Suddenly, a gun barrel was pointed straight at him.

"Kaz, please! Help me!"

He had to save Tiffany. He staggered forward, watching for the flash of polished steel. The hand with the gun came down at him. Kaz lashed out with his foot. He connected squarely with the hand.

A female cry rose in the trees. The gun fell to the ground, landing at Kaz's feet. He reached down, grabbing the gun in his right hand.

He lifted the pistol and pointed it at the girls. "Stop it!"

Suddenly they broke apart. The identical faces turned to stare at him. In the darkness, he couldn't tell the difference between them.

"Tiffany!"

"Yes, Kaz. I'm here."

The words had come from the girl on the left.

"No," said the girl on the right. "Don't trust her, Kaz."

Kaz squinted at both of them. He was confused. He had to be sure before he made a move.

His eyes fell on the girl to the left. "If you're Tiffany, then what did we have for dinner the night I came to your father's house?"

"Chinese food!"

He smiled. "Okay, you're Tiffany. Get over here next to me."

Tiffany slipped beside him. "Are you all right? I've been so worried about you."

"Please," Melanie whined. "You don't understand, Kaz."

He glared at her. "Don't understand? I understand that you killed Carol and Sally and Marcia. And Ricky!"

"No!" Melanie cried. "Ricky and I were out on a date. We just—"

"It's over," Kaz said. "You're finished, Melanie."

Tiffany touched his right arm. "Give me the gun, Kaz. I'll hold it on her while you tie her up."

Melanie tried to take a step toward them. "Don't listen to her, Kaz. You've got to—"

"Shut up, thief," Tiffany cried.

Kaz was starting to feel weak. He had been through too much during the past twenty-four hours. His hand was trembling. Maybe he should give the gun to Tiffany while he still had some strength left.

"Here," he said, handing the gun to Tiffany. "Take it."

She took the gun from his hand. Kaz slumped to the ground. His head was spinning. He felt soft hands caressing his cheeks.

"Kaz. Oh, my sweetheart."

He gazed up at the beautiful face. "Tiffany—"

"No, I'm Melanie. You shouldn't have given her the gun, love-puppy. She's the one who killed those girls."

Kaz couldn't believe what he was hearing. "No, Tiffany didn't—"

"Yes, I did," Tiffany said, pointing the gun at them. "And now I'm going to kill both of you!"

# Chapter 20

Kaz gaped up at the bore of the pistol in Tiffany's hand. "No, you can't—"

"Yes, I can. And I did, lover boy. You thought you'd two-time me with the others, but I showed you."

He reached out toward her. "Tiffany, please—"

Melanie shook her head. "She's gone. She lost it."

"Shut up!" Tiffany cried. "Shut your vulgar mouth!"

"How did you get out here?" Kaz asked.

"I followed my sister and her new boyfriend," Tiffany went on. "They were coming out here to have some fun. I knew you had been seeing my sister, Kaz. I figured it out, the same way I figured out the others. I saw you and Carol arguing in the hall. I heard Sally talking about you at the record store. Are you happy now, Kaz? Just like my father. You couldn't leave the girls alone, could you?"

"She's crazy," Melanie whispered.

"Shut up!"

"Please," Kaz said. "There's no need to kill us."

"I thought you were different," Tiffany said. "But you were just like the rest. So I evened the score. I followed Melanie in my father's Porsche. It's on the other side of the ice cream stand. I didn't expect to find your little friend Marcia. She was a lucky break. But there she was, talking to you on the phone. You were seeing her, too, weren't you, lover boy? She finally achieved her martyrdom. Carol, Sally, Marcia, Melanie. But you didn't fool me."

"You left the yearbook in my room," Kaz said.

"Yes, that was me. I wanted you to come to Sally's that night. I was going to kill you both and make it look like a murder/suicide. But you were late, Kaz. So I had to kill Sally first. She was the toughest. She really put up a fight."

Melanie shuddered. "You're gross."

"I told you to shut up!"

A maniacal gleam shone in Tiffany's killer eyes. She seemed to be enjoying her moment of triumph. She was going to kill them as the final act of her morbid drama.

"Why?" Kaz muttered. "Why did you kill them?"

Tiffany laughed demonically. "I killed Ricky because he was out with Melanie. He just got in the way. I killed the others because they were tramps, just like my dear mother. They wanted to take you away from me. But they couldn't. I showed them."

"You didn't show anyone!" Melanie cried. "You'll never get away with this."

"Yes I will! I'll tell the police how you and Kaz kidnapped me. You were both in on the plot to kill those girls."

"It'll never work," Melanie challenged.

"Kaz is already wanted by the sheriff," Tiffany replied. "It will be easy to frame him."

"What about Ricky?" Kaz asked. "How will you explain him? And Marcia?"

Tiffany thought about it for a moment. "I'll just say you killed them for the same reason you killed Carol and Sally—for the fun of it."

Melanie scoffed. "No one will buy that."

"Yes, they will. I'll cry pitifully. They'll believe me. I'm not like you, sister dear. I have a spotless reputation. I'll say you and Kaz got in a fight while you were deciding how to kill me. I'll say I escaped. Then they'll think that Kaz killed you, Melanie. Then he killed himself. It'll be great."

Kaz coughed. "Tiffany, don't do it. You don't want to kill again. Melanie is your sister. And I loved you, Tiff. I—"

"Don't ever call me that! Do you hear? Never call me that!"

"She's fried," Melanie whispered. "Just go along with her. We might get a chance."

"Stand up," Tiffany commanded. "Get on your feet." She moved closer to them, waving the gun. "Stand up or I'll kill you right now!"

Melanie rose from the ground. She helped Kaz to his feet. He was weak, but he was still able to maintain his balance. He had to lean on Melanie when Tiffany told them to walk.

Holding the gun on them, Tiffany forced them through the woods. They staggered under the glow of the moon. Kaz could hear something roaring in the distance. When they emerged at the edge of the cliffs, he realized it was the lapping surf at Lighthouse Bay.

"It's a long drop," Tiffany said. "They'll find you floating in the bay. Murder/suicide. That's what the papers will say."

Melanie wasn't ready to give up. "Go on, Tiffany. Shoot us. Kill us both if you have the guts."

Kaz gaped at her. "Melanie!"

"You shut up, Kaz," Melanie went on. "You got us into this. I cared about you, but it wasn't enough. You had to have the others. It's all your fault. You reminded my sister of our dear daddy. That's what made her go bonkers. Isn't that right, *Tiff?*"

The hateful scowl spread over Tiffany's face. "Shut up, Melanie. Shut your mouth!"

Melanie took a bold step forward. "Oh yeah, *Tiff!* How about it, *Tiff?* Isn't that what our dear father always called you? Remember how he used to come into our room, *Tiff?* How about it, *Tiff?*"

Tiffany grabbed her head with one hand. "Shut up!"

"Our dear daddy," Melanie went on, inching closer. "You went with him after the divorce. Did he come up the stairs in the dark? Did he creep—?"

"No, you're lying. He never did that."

"I'm telling the truth!" Melanie cried. "You know why I went with Mom. Sure, she drinks. But she didn't start until she found out what was really going on. You tried to cover for him by denying it, but she knew the truth."

Tiffany raised the gun with her trembling hand. "I have to kill you, Melanie. I have to do it."

Melanie kept sliding forward. "Our little secret. Isn't that what Daddy used to say, *Tiff?* 'Don't tell Mom, *Tiff!* It's our little secret.' I hate his guts. You should have killed *him* instead of those girls!"

"You have to die. I can't listen to your lies."

"No!" Kaz cried. "Don't—"

Tiffany's finger tightened on the trigger. "Good-bye, liar!"

She pulled the trigger. The hammer clicked harmlessly. She pulled the trigger again, and the same thing happened.

"Is that the gun from Daddy's Porsche?" asked Melanie.

"Yes," Tiffany answered, with panic in her voice. "He just got it six months ago."

Melanie walked toward her sister. She started to laugh. "You poor fool. I stole the clip from that gun just after I heard Daddy bought it. I don't like people having guns."

A furious expression gripped Tiffany's gorgeous features. She turned toward the ocean, far below, and tossed the gun with all her might. Then, with her silken hair blowing gently in the breeze, she leapt into the void.


"All right, Kasden," Sheriff Hagen said. "Let's go over it one more time."

Kaz was in his parents' living room, sitting on the couch. The sheriff was finding Mr. Kasden's easy chair much to his liking. Kaz had already told him once about what had happened.

"Tiffany Kaylor killed those girls," he said again. "I was dating her. She was jealous. There was also something weird between her and her father. She lost it."

Hagen sighed. "I found two more bodies out at Creighton Woods. Buller and the Granholm girl."

"Marcia was trying to help me," Kaz replied. "Just like I told you. Tiffany was following her sister. She wanted to kill her. Marcia and Ricky just got in the way. Marcia wanted to help me. Ricky and Melanie were on a date. Ask Melanie."

"We did," Hagen replied. "I talked to her yesterday. You two have your story down pretty good. I had my men search Lighthouse Bay, but we haven't been able to find Melanie's sister."

"She went off the cliff," Kaz replied. "I swear."

Hagen shook his head. "You kids better not be lying. I'm leaving now. But I'll be back. And there's a guard outside. He'll be there as long as your story remains unconfirmed, Kasden."

"Sheriff, you've got to believe me. I swear I'm telling the truth."

Hagen sighed. "For your sake, I hope you are."

After the sheriff was gone, Kaz ate a quiet meal with his parents. It was all over, and they were all relieved, but Kaz knew he would never be the same.

Kaz didn't want to watch television. He didn't want to read or study. He just wanted to sit in his room and dream. He couldn't get Tiffany out of his mind. Sitting in his chair by the window, he drifted off to sleep.

Suddenly she was in front of him.

"Tiffany!"

"Hello, lover boy."

"How did you get here?"

"I'm a great swimmer, Kaz. Now it's time for you to die!"

She reached under her skirt and pulled out a long-bladed knife. Kaz's arms were like lead weights.

Kaz had to roll away from her. He fell out of the chair onto the floor. He had escaped the first thrust, but she was coming after him.

He reached up toward her. The blade came down. The sharp point caught his shoulder. Blood gushed from the wound.

"Lover boy!"

She raised the blade again. Kaz lashed out with his feet. He caught her legs with the kick. Tiffany went down on the floor.

Kaz tried to stand up. Tiffany swung the blade, cutting his calf. Kaz began to crawl away from her, leaving a blood trail on the floor.

"I'm going to kill you, lover boy."

Tiffany had scrambled to her feet. She stalked him across the floor, making panting noises. She looked more beautiful than ever. Kaz wanted to wake up. He had to escape from the dream. The pains in his body were too real.

"You were a heartbreaker," Tiffany cried. "I'm going to cut out your heart!"

Kaz couldn't retreat any farther. The mad girl approached him slowly. He tried to kick her again, but she was ready for him this time.

"You can't hurt me, lover boy. Heartbreaker, I'm going to cut your heart in two!"

She lifted the blade high. Kaz saw the reflection in the dim night light. He tried to raise his hand. "Heartbreaker!"

# Chapter 21

"Easy," Melanie said. "It's me, not my crazy sister. Your mother said I could come up."

Sweat broke on Kaz's face. He opened his eyes.

"What a nightmare you must have been having," Melanie said.

Kaz sighed. "It was incredible."

Melanie shook her head. "My sister had a way of getting into your dreams."

Kaz saw that Melanie was wearing one of her nicest outfits. "How are you?"

She shrugged. "Okay."

"So Hagen's finally believing us?" he asked.

She nodded. "Tiffany's body washing up didn't hurt things any."

"When did they find her?"

"About an hour ago. She came up with a fishnet," Melanie replied.

Kaz squinted at her. "We had some fun together, didn't we?"

Her eyes narrowed. "You had fun with Tiffany, too."

"Didn't take you long to go out with Ricky Buller after I—"

"I was just trying to forget about you!" she cried.

"Do you hate me?" he asked.

"Yes, but I'll get over it," she replied. "How about you?"

"You're my friend, Melanie. I care about you. When we get back to school—"

"I'm dropping out," Melanie said quickly. "I can't go back to Cresswell. Not after—I mean, I've had it with school anyway."

"You could finish up at night school," Kaz offered. "Or take the test for the equivalency diploma."

"Maybe. I never pictured myself as the academic type. At least its time to leave Cresswell."

"You saved me out there at the cliffs. If you hadn't . . . she would have killed us both."

Melanie shuddered.

"She was smart to fool everyone like that," Kaz went on. "I'm sorry I got involved with her. I'm sorry for everyone. Carol, Marcia, Sally. Their parents. Sally's aunt. Ricky, too. He didn't deserve that."

"No, he didn't."

A tear rolled down his cheek. "Why did I fall for her?"

Melanie tried to smile. "Because she looks like me! You had the best, you just wanted to try the rest, Kaz."

He shook his head. "Call me Wayne. I don't like Kaz anymore."

"Okay, Wayne. Hey, let's go for a ride. I'll buy you a cheeseburger."

"Are you sure you can't steal it?"

"Not this time," she said, taking his hand.

He looked at her. She was so beautiful. But that no longer mattered to him. He only cared about what was inside her. They had both been hurt too much. Maybe they could help each other with the healing.

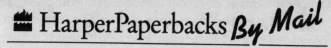